MW00811514

BETRAYAL AT THE BEACH

DANGEROUS CURVES #1

K.L. MONTGOMERY

MOUNTAINS WANTED

Cover design by the author, made with images licensed through
DepositPhotos.
Paperback ISBN: 978-1-949394-29-0

Published by Mountains Wanted Publishing
P.O. Box 1014
Georgetown, DE 19947
mountainswanted.com

Created with Vellum

To all my readers who push me to keep going, to try new things, and who are supportive no matter what.

ONE

My favorite patron, thirteen-year-old Anna Cooper, carefully made her way to my desk with a towering stack of books, which she set down right in front of me with a huge, triumphant grin on her face.

I eyed the stack—she had a good mix of classics and newer stuff. She liked paranormal and dystopian books the best, but I'd steered her toward a couple of series I enjoyed as a teen. I hated to think those were considered classics now...but...yeah, they were. No getting around that.

"Planning on reading this weekend?" I scanned the first book's barcode, then the next, quickly making my way through the whole stack.

"Just a little." She wouldn't stop beaming, except when her glasses slid down her cute button nose, and she had to push them back up again. I noticed she'd gotten braces since the last time I saw her. "You have something to do with that?" She pointed at the huge banner hanging over the opening to the adult section.

Friends of Bryce Beach Public Library Annual Gala
Join us Saturday, April 27th at 7 pm
for dinner, dancing & magic.
Books are a uniquely portable magic.
Support your community library!

I glanced up at the banner I created myself with my mad graphic design skills. "Yep, I'm the Librarian Liaison to the Friends of the Library," I announced.

Last year I merely helped out, but apparently I impressed the right people because, this year, I was named head of the planning committee. "It's just a fancy way of saying I'm in charge of the annual gala. I can't believe it's tonight. Finally! We've been working really hard on it." I pretended to wipe sweat off my brow to emphasize all the hard work.

Anna's eyes grew round as she looked at the banner again and then back at me. She tucked a few of her dark brown braids behind her ear. "'Gala' sounds fancy. Do you have to get dressed up? What are you wearing?"

I'd never known my favorite patron to take an interest in fashion, but teens were always reinventing themselves. "Eh, 'gala' is just a euphemism for fundraiser." I waved my hand dismissively. "Basically, the Friends of the Library invite as many rich people as they can to the gala and try to convince them to give money to the library. They can write the donations off on their taxes, so it's a win-win!"

My young friend smirked. "I figured as much. I hope they give lots and lots this year so you can buy lots and lots of new books!"

"Me too!" I assured her.

And to help achieve that outcome, I had everything crossed: fingers, toes, and whatever other body parts were crossable—*eyes?* We needed to make a lot of money this year because our budget was slashed by the town council last year, and I had a whole backlist of things I wanted to order as soon as this money cleared the bank. I was going on a major shopping spree, and I couldn't wait!

Buying books was now my favorite past-time—ever since I gave up on baking. No matter how closely I followed the recipe, everything I baked turned out to be an epic disaster. And no one would let me forget it. *Especially considering my last name is Baker.*

Anna brought me out of my book-buying fantasy with her next question: "So, what are you wearing, then?" She leaned toward the desk to collect the stack of books I'd just checked out to her, then stuffed them into the canvas bag she was wearing over her shoulder.

I sighed. "Um, good question."

I hadn't really thought that far ahead yet. I'd been busy worrying about the caterers and the entertainment (a magician to go with the theme—I wasn't a big fan of the idea, but the Friends of the Library, particularly the mayor's wife, *insisted*) and making sure my boss wouldn't yell at me for screwing something up. She expected nothing less than perfection at all times. It felt like no matter how carefully I planned, something—even a tiny little trivial detail—would inevitably go wrong.

"Do you have any nice dresses?" Anna pressed.

"Nice dresses," I repeated like it was a foreign phrase rolling off my tongue for the first time. "Well, I have the dresses I wear to work and church. Guess I'll just wear one of those." I shrugged because my gala outfit was down at the very bottom of my priority list.

Anna's nose wrinkled up as she fixed her gaze on me. "I think you can do better than that, Ms. Baker."

I bit my lip to avoid laughing because the seriousness on her face was epic. "Anna, my dear, I do appreciate your concern, but I'm a fluffy forty-two-year-old librarian who's never been married. And though I'm completely fabulous in many ways, I haven't worn a fancy dress since my high school prom, and I probably never will."

An apology showed up in the downturn of her lips and furrowing of her brows. "I'm sorry. I shouldn't be harassing you about your clothes," her face brightened, "but I could totally see you in a pretty red dress. Hope you'll take some pictures of the gala for the library's social media accounts. It sounds like fun...you know, if you're into that sort of thing." She gestured to her bookbag. "I'd still rather be home reading."

She wasn't the only one. "Thanks, and of course I will." A smile crept across my face at her earnestness. She was an old soul in a tiny teenager's body. "And I'm sure I'll find something suitable to wear."

"You can't actually be forty-two," Anna continued, completely straight-faced. "I would have said thirty-five at the oldest."

Now I was laughing. Teenagers almost always gave it to you straight; I liked that about them. They were a tough crowd sometimes, but I adored working with them. I loved my job as a Young Adult librarian, and I couldn't imagine doing anything else.

"I hope you enjoy your weekend," I told her as she turned to head for the door with a spring in her step. She could tell she'd made my day, and she seemed a little high on the victory. I loved that for her. And me. I could be a cranky, moody chick from time to time—despite my first name—but I really did enjoy my teens. Particularly Miss Anna Cooper. They kept me young.

"Oh, don't you worry! I will!" she called over her shoulder, her new braces sparkling in her wide grin. "Good luck with the gala!"

"I'll post lots of pics," I promised, waving to her. Then I turned back to my list of approximately four million things I needed to do and added one more bullet point at the very bottom: *find something to wear.*

※

I'd gotten home from work late, of course, which meant I had even less time to tackle that last-minute addition to my to-do list: the wardrobe conundrum. I threw my bag down on the kitchen table and was immediately assaulted by my two cats: Bond, my male tuxedo cat, named after James Bond (naturally); and my female long-haired calico, Paige, full name Paige Turner (because I'm a super clever librarian). She also refused to answer to a plethora of nicknames: Paigie-Poo, Pooh Bear, Paigie Patootie, and my personal favorite, Paigella DeVille, which she earned when she was being less than cuddly and congenial.

"Hi, yes, I missed you too!" I cooed as I rubbed their furry little faces in tandem. This was why God gave me two hands. I was sure of it.

I scooped their food into their respective dishes and patted them both on the heads before they scurried over to sample the flavor of the day. Fish. *Ewww*. The smell lingered in the air as I rushed down the hall to the bathroom.

I lived in a quaint little wood-shingled cottage not far from the beach, though nobody was that far from the water in our small coastal town of Bryce Beach, named after Nathaniel Bryce. He and his crew of men sailed from England in 1637. They were aiming for the Massachusetts colony when they were blown off-course and ended up quite a bit farther south. Like the Puritans and Pilgrims, the Bryce Beach founders were pursuing religious liberty, which took them on their treacherous journey across the Atlantic.

The library where I worked, aptly named Bryce Beach Public Library, boasted a prized possession: a Bible that dated back to the very first church established in town, and it was signed by none other than Nathaniel Bryce and the other founding fathers, the five surviving men he'd been shipwrecked with just off the coast. They swam to shore, set up a little village, and the rest is history! Like, *literally* history! Every kid who grows up in Bryce Beach learns the story by the time they're in fourth grade.

I turned on the shower, and while waiting for it to

warm up, I bravely marched to my closet to secure a garment for tonight's event. I pushed hanger after hanger farther and farther back on the rack after eliminating most of my dresses. Too short. Too tight. Too flowery. Too polka-dotty. Then, finally, it was like God sent a choir of angels to serenade me, because I was pretty sure I heard a heavenly "Ahhhhh!" as a halo of light shimmered around a pretty cranberry-red dress I'd forgotten I even owned.

Didn't Anna say I would look lovely in red? I remembered, pulling it off the hanger and holding it up to my body. Wondering what the chances were that it would actually fit me, I threw it on the bed to await its fate while I took my shower.

When I returned ten minutes later, it was still there, looking up at me like Cinderella begging to go to the ball. I toweled off, slid the dress up, and lo and behold, like some sort of miracle, it zipped right up. I was right. This dress was the product of divine intervention; I just knew it.

Standing in front of the full-length mirror, I checked out the fit. I was never what I would call *happy* with my body in any outfit, but to my surprise, this dress wasn't half bad. Which is to say I looked sorta good. *Alright, that might be pushing it.* I definitely looked okay. *Super okay!*

I brushed out my frizzy red curls, scrunched them with some curl cream, then hastily redid my makeup, knowing any second my doorbell would ring. My coworkers and best friends, Molly and Evangeline, were picking me up any minute, and they would get on my case if I was still fussing with my hair and makeup.

I'd only achieved half a smoky eye when the doorbell

ding-donged at the front of the house. I scurried in my bare feet—I hadn't yet tackled the footwear issue—to open the door, though if I waited long enough, they'd surely show themselves in.

"You're not ready yet!" Evangeline screeched. "I told you, Molly." Her hands flew to her slim hips as her lips drew themselves into a tight purse.

I wasn't exactly Miss Mary Sunshine, despite my name, but my colleague Evangeline was even grumpier than me. We considered it an endearing quality. If we were Care Bears, she'd be Grumpy Bear. Plus, if I were a cataloguer, I'd probably be grumpy too. I barely passed my cataloging class in library school. I couldn't imagine doing it for eight hours a day! It required a level of patience and meticulousness the Good Lord did not bless me with.

Molly, who was the polar opposite of Evangeline, with long, wavy blonde hair and a full, curvy figure like my own, turned her pale blue eyes to me, sweeping them down my body. "Oh, I love your dress! You look amazing, Sunshine!"

"Thanks, Molls!" I twirled around, relishing the way the silky red fabric lifted and swished around my thighs. If I wasn't careful walking over a subway grate, I could very well have a Marilyn Monroe *Seven Year Itch* moment. Fortunately, we didn't have a subway in Bryce Beach. I didn't even think we had a bus or a taxi.

How could I buy myself some time? *Oh, I know...*

"Hey, there are some cookies on the counter if you want a snack while you wait," I plied them.

A look of horror crept across Molly's face, while

Evangeline stifled a chuckle. "Cookies you baked?" the former asked, her voice wavering with trepidation.

I rolled my eyes. "They're from the bakery on the boardwalk."

My baking fiascos were well known. For most of my thirties, I tried my hardest to live up to my surname, Baker. My mother was a wonderful baker—people clamored for her famous chocolate fudge three-layer cake three towns over. My Grandma Baker's pies regularly took home blue ribbons from the county fair. But my attempts always ended in utter disaster. When I turned forty, I finally gave up on ever mastering baking. Heck, I couldn't even claim beginner status. No wonder I hadn't ever snagged a husband!

"Well, are you gonna go finish getting ready or what?" Evangeline growled as she examined her nails. They were usually painted black to match her goth aesthetic, but she'd changed her nail polish to echo her purple dress.

"Hello to you too," I called over my shoulder as I pranced back down the hall. Could I get away without wearing shoes? I knew my friends were going to insist on heels to go with this epic dress, and I was already dreading them with every fiber of my being.

I finished my eye makeup and swept on some lip gloss before giving myself a final once-over in the bathroom mirror. It was as good as it was gonna get. Thankfully, no one would be paying attention to me tonight—not like they ever did. Despite my red hair and mouthy nature, I tended to fade right into the background. Besides, the goal was to bring in as much money as possible for the library. Nothing mattered except every-thing going smoothly with NO hiccups.

After grabbing my coat and purse off the sofa, I turned to my posse. "Well, ladies, are we ready?"

"Sunshine Baker!" Evangeline broke out my full name. "Where in the world do you think you are going with no shoes?"

I glanced down at my still bare feet. "Oh, yeah."

Molly laughed as I tiptoed to the closet in my foyer and pulled out a very sensible pair of black flats. Then she adamantly shook her head and broke out the same line Anna Cooper used on me earlier today: "I think you can do better than that!"

Evangeline was tapping her toe against my hardwood floor. She must use all her patience up on cataloging books. It was such a tedious process, after all.

"Grab some heels, and let's go, Sunshine," she urged me. "You don't want to be late to your own event!"

She had a point there. "I don't think wearing heels is a good idea," I protested. "My feet will hurt, and what if I need to run around and solve problems? Like a fixer! I might have to go into fixer mode."

Molly was still laughing as I went head to head with Evangeline. Our blonde friend always stepped back and watched the show, never one to get involved in our squab-bles. She had a gentle, fun-loving, kind spirit, which served her well as our children's librarian. She was also very obviously a middle child, whereas Evangeline and I were both headstrong firstborns.

"Fine. Wear the flats but take heels to change into during the dinner and speech portion of the evening,"

Evangeline suggested, smoothing her jet-black hair over her shoulder. "Now who's the fixer?" Her lips curled into a smug smirk.

"Great idea!" I grabbed a pair of strappy silver kitten heels, stuffed them into my bag, and we were off. Now to pray for no hiccups. God came to my aid with my wardrobe dilemma, surely He could prevent any issues from cropping up tonight.

I'd played so many scenarios through my head when it came to this event, but the bottom line was this: if we didn't collect enough donations to offset the city's budget cuts, my wardrobe would be the least of my problems. I had a feeling, among the entire library staff, the YA Librarian was the least valued position. *After all, teens don't even use the library anymore, right?* That was what people thought, anyway.

I couldn't lose my job! I had bills to pay and two feline mouths to feed. And probably waaaaay too much pride. That was something I was working on, and I was sure I could get it under control without something so drastic as getting fired.

Right, Lord?

TWO

When we arrived at the library, I took a deep breath, offering up my final prayer for a successful evening. *Okay, it probably wasn't going to be my final one—let's be realistic.* I tried not to be one of those Christians who only prayed when I needed something, but, wow, I was probably really pushing it with the number I'd sent up just since this afternoon. *I promise I'll make it up to you, Father,* I said silently as I walked up the steps in my comfy flats.

Our boss, Susan Gooch, was standing just inside the building in the vestibule that led from the entrance to the lobby. She barely looked up at us as she arranged a balloon bouquet on a welcome table filled with nametags. Her short-cropped silver hair shone under the lights like a halo encircling her head.

"Oh, you're here," she snapped when she finally acknowledged our presence. "I'll let you finish this project." Then she slipped into the building via one of the two heavy wooden doors before I could even get one word out of my mouth.

"Wow, what crawled up her behind?" Evangeline rolled her eyes.

My quick-on-the-draw shushing finger immediately flew to my lips, even though there was zero chance my friend's snarky comment passed through the thick wood doors. The Director of the Library was brusque and analytical, and could come across cold at times, but she was efficient and ran a tight ship. She didn't put up with any shenanigans from her staff—or from patrons, for that matter. It was good to know she was on my side whenever I had to deal with surly adolescent patrons, which did happen from time to time, even if I did consider myself a professional teen wrangler.

As I was finishing arranging the nametags for guests in perfect alphabetical order, the doors swung open, and our Head of Reference, Tom Watson, strolled in with his wife on his arm, and right behind him was our Head of Circulation, Barbara Jensen, with her husband in tow.

"Good evening! Welcome to the gala!" I practiced my smile for when I'd be greeting the real guests—rich people who would hopefully give us lots of money. I would probably get stuck in the role of official greeter, though if I were lucky, one of the Friends of the Library board members would recognize they needed a prettier, more gregarious personality for such an important task.

"What's up?" Tom asked, a rhetorical question I knew he didn't want an actual answer to.

"Hi, Sunshine," his wife said, and I nodded in acknowledgment.

"Do you need me to do anything?" Barbara asked as she stepped inside, her husband right on her heels.

"Can you just sweep the first floor and make sure everything looks perfect?" I followed up my request with a sparkling smile.

"Will do!" Barbara's gray curls shook around her face as she nodded. She was about the same age as Susan and had an efficient nature too, but she was much warmer and more nurturing than our boss.

Soon the vestibule was empty, and Molly and Evangeline peered through the glass of the two wooden doors, gazing longingly at the pending festivities. The magician was setting up and would soon be dazzling everyone with his act. They obviously didn't want to sit out here with me and miss all the fun.

"Go on," I urged my friends, releasing them from their unofficial duty of keeping me company. "I'll be okay out here on my own...and even if I get lonely, I'll have that tiny cricket over there in the corner." I pointed to the little guy, who immediately scurried away when everyone's eyes shifted to him.

"I'll stay with you," Molly said, a genuine smile accompanying her offer. "I don't mind."

Evangeline shrugged. She was not known for being particularly sociable, but she seemed determined to get this party over with. "I'm going in." She took a deep breath of resolve and swung open one of the double doors. The music from the DJ the committee had hired seeped through the crack in the door until it clicked shut next to its twin.

Together, Molly and I tackled greeting duties,

welcoming the mayor and his wife; Mr. and Mrs. James, the Chief of Bryce Beach Police's parents; the biggest library supporter in town, Ms. Willa Bryce Monroe; most of the members of the Friends of the Library committee and their plus-ones; and several other townspeople. Most notable among the townspeople were Mr. and Mrs. Phillip Baker, AKA my mom and dad.

My mother's hip must have been acting up because she was walking with a bit of a lurch as my father practically dragged her up the library steps. They were quite a pair, my parents. Reformed hippies—who else would name their daughter Sunshine and their son River?—they were enjoying their retirement and supporting causes that were important to them, and sometimes those causes opposed each other, as my parents tended to have divergent views when it came to, well, everything. How they'd been married for forty-five years was nothing short of a miracle and, as far as I was concerned, definitive proof of God's existence.

"Well, if my daughter isn't the prettiest girl in town tonight in her red dress!" my mother cooed as she straightened her slumped posture and took her first full look at me.

"Mom, you haven't even been inside yet." I huffed out a sigh. She was always over-the-top positive. No wonder she chose to name me Sunshine—she probably thought I'd follow in her bright, shiny footsteps.

"Hi, Mrs. Baker!" Molly gushed from beside me. She thought my parents were "the most adorable couple ever." She'd clearly never heard one of their political debates.

"Hey, Molly! You look pretty tonight too. Blue is your color," my mom gushed.

"You guys didn't have to come, you know," I said, meeting my dad's eyes. "You already donate to a lot of causes, and you're retired now, so—"

"This is one cause we can actually agree on!" he joked, tipping an imaginary hat at my best friend, who giggled as he escorted my mother through the doors.

"Those two are hashtag relationship goals," Molly swooned, dramatically sweeping her hand across her blonde brow.

"Oh, please. Unless you want to bicker about every single election, every environmental issue, every social issue, every economic issue—" I rolled my eyes. "Are you sensing a theme here?"

"I still think they're adorable," Molly maintained. "And there's nothing you can say to convince me otherwise."

Neither Molly nor I were married, and I was surprised my mother didn't make a comment about one or both of us finding the elusive Man of Our Dreams at tonight's event. Maybe she finally realized, like Molly and I had both accepted, the marriage ship had sailed long ago. It probably sailed right out of Bryce Cove and into the Atlantic, headed for bluer waters. That would be the nautical version of "greener pastures," right? I thought so.

Right after my parents headed inside, a flash of fuchsia bolted by.

"Was that Jada?" I asked, my head whipping back toward Molly.

"Hey!" Molly called after her, and the petite fuchsia-clad woman with a crown of amber-colored corkscrew curls froze in place before slowly turning to face us.

"Hi," she sighed. "I'm late, sorry. I was just trying to sneak in!"

"At least let us grab your nametag for you first," I implored, scanning the table for "Jada Booker." If anyone was meant to work in a library, I was pretty sure it was our colleague Jada, who was fresh out of library school and our new Director of Technical Services. She'd worked in an academic periodicals department for several years before deciding to go for her master's degree.

"Thanks, guys." She gave us a little wave before heading inside.

"Hey, do you mind watching the table for a few while I see how things are going?" I asked Molly when the steady stream of incoming partygoers seemed to trickle down to nothing.

"Sure, of course." She smiled and nodded in agreement as she smoothed down her navy blue dress and patted her glossy blonde waves.

I spent about half a second considering putting on the heels I'd stashed under the table, then I headed inside in my comfy flats, my eyes darting around the room as I took in all the decorations, the music, and the smell of excitement in the air. Everything looked perfect! I just wanted to let out a giant "Squeee!" and pat myself on the back for all my hard work paying off. Of course, there was still plenty of time for things to go sideways, but at least right now... I was going to bask in my victory for a moment.

As I was basking, I picked up on a palpable energy

circulating through the room. Everyone was dressed to the nines and wore smiles that sparkled brighter than the blingiest bling. The magician had just finished his first act and was putting away some of his props. Judging from the looks on everyone's faces, they'd been impressed with his performance. I still didn't get the draw, and I thought magicians were more for kids than adults, but I was glad it was a hit with the guests.

"There you are, Sunshine!" came a voice from behind me, startling me out of basking mode.

I whipped around to see two members of the Friends of the Library committee, Rosita Rodriquez and Heather Birch. They were both tall and model-thin. Rosita wore her long brown hair with golden blonde highlights in perfect ringlets, and Heather's ash-blonde hair was swept up in a French twist with curtain bangs framing her heart-shaped face. They must have thought they were coming to the adult version of prom because they were both decked out in what could only be described as formal gowns. Rosita's was pink with pearl and sequin spangles glittering in the dim light, and Heather's hugged her body so tightly, one wrong move, and the structural integrity of those seams would be put to the ultimate test.

"Hi there. Is everything okay?" I didn't know why I automatically assumed there must be a problem if they were deigning to speak with me. It might have been some sort of holdover from high school when the uber-popular folks routinely avoided chubby band geeks such as myself. I might have been forty-two years old, but some days the ghosts of my youth were still very much alive and kicking.

No wonder I'd chosen to become a librarian who works with young adults. I knew many of my patrons were just like me when I was coming of age. I loved books and the library then too. Books were my refuge. That was why my job and this event were both so important. So I plastered on a smile and waited to see if the Barbie twins needed anything from me.

"The place looks great!" Heather schmoozed. She turned to say something to Rosita when another woman sidled up between them, wrapping her arms around both of their waists and bringing Barbie #1 and Barbie #2's faces to rest on either side of hers.

The Barbies squealed as the mayor's wife planted light smooches on both of their cheeks—heaven forbid she muss their makeup, which was no doubt professionally applied. "What's up, girls?"

The mayor's wife, Camille Steyer, was probably a decade older than Rosita and Heather, but she pretended they were three peas in a pod. She was dressed a little more conservatively in a floor-length purple maxi dress, a sparkling diamond choker around her slim, elegant neck. Her golden blonde mane fell around her bare shoulders, looking glossy and ironed perfectly straight for the occasion.

"Hi, Sunshine," she greeted me. I was surprised she remembered my name, even though I was the library liaison to the committee she was the chairwoman of—and my name was pretty hard to forget.

"Hi, Camille. Everything seems to be going smoothly." I glanced around, hoping not to find anything that would contradict my statement.

"Yes, yes! I made sure the caterers are all on task. Dinner will be served in the activities room in fifteen minutes," she said. "My husband has a wonderful speech planned! You'll be giving him an introduction, won't you?"

My stomach leapt into my throat, apparently hoping to make a quick escape out my mouth. I swallowed down the sour saliva that was stirred up and settled my gaze on Camille Steyer. "I'll be doing what, now?"

Her heavily glossed lips pressed together as her sharp blue stare pierced into me. "The library liaison always introduces the speakers at the annual gala," she said as though I were the dumbest person in the world for not knowing this obvious fact.

My heart pounded into my ribcage like it was also trying to make a break for it. "I was under the impression it was the library director's job?"

I didn't mean to make it sound like a question. I was trying to sound assertive and sure of myself, but I failed miserably, as evidenced by the smug grins that crept across all three of their faces. They were definitely enjoying the show. I was sure the color had drained from my face, and my limbs were visibly shaking at the prospect of forced public speaking.

"No, it's all you, sweetie," Rosita assured me, giving me a patronizing pat on the arm.

I had a few phobias, and *glossophobia* was number one on my list:

5. Spiders
4. Tight, confined spaces

3. Getting into a serious accident while wearing old,
holey underwear (thanks for that one, Mom!)

2. Clowns

1. Public speaking

I'd been waiting for something to ruin an otherwise perfect evening. I guessed it was going to be this. How in the world was I going to pull this off with only fifteen minutes' notice?

Jesus, take the wheel!

❦

I had, in the past, been accused of having pluck, moxie, spunk or whatever euphemism was commonly used for women who speak their minds. Sucking in a deep breath, I girded my loins and reached deep within to muster up whatever measure of that quality was buried inside me because I was going to need it to get through this brush with death. *I mean public speaking.*

While the other members of the gala planning committee were herding the cats, *I mean guests,* to the activities room on the second floor, I rushed up there to check the room set-up. I found my boss, Susan, hooking up the podium and turning on the projector.

My heart leapt for joy. Maybe Susan would intervene! *So, God, what do You say? Can we make that happen?*

"Hey, it's going well so far, isn't it?" My voice came out so chipper, it almost sounded like my parents gave me the right name after all.

"Could definitely be worse," she sort of agreed with me? "You need the microphone for this, or can you project your voice?" She held up the wireless mic and pinned her dark gaze on me.

"Oh, right. Well, about that..." my voice trailed off as I scrambled for a good excuse to get out of this task. "Don't you think the introductions would come better from you? I mean, you're the Library Director, after all. Who am I but an unimportant foot soldier? You're *Le Général!*" I pretended to have a French accent. Badly.

"I'm sure you can manage," Susan said, crushing my dreams of keeping my heart from exploding tonight.

Alright, I told myself. *I can do this.* What was that Bible verse? *I can do all things through Christ who strengthens me?* Oh, yeah, I totally had this.

Then, as people began to filter into the room, I watched my parents' faces light up when they saw I had the microphone and was standing behind the podium poised to speak. I had to make them proud.

Molly shot me a look from the corner that said, "You go, girl!" and Evangeline leaned against the wall, arms crossed over her chest with a bored expression all over her face. That was as supportive as she got. At least she was here, right? As much as she hated crowds, it really was a genuine show of friendship.

Then, out of nowhere, someone in a suit handed me an index card, and on it was written an introduction for the mayor. All I had to do was read it. I was saved! *Yes! I can read. My whole job is based on reading!*

All eyes were on me as a hush fell over the room. I sucked in a deep breath and sent up one last prayer before addressing the crowd. "Thank you all for coming out tonight to support the Bryce Beach Public Library. I'm Sunshine Baker, the Young Adult Librarian here at BBPL. On behalf of our director, Ms. Susan Gooch, and the rest of the BBPL staff, welcome to our annual gala."

A thunderous applause rose up from the crowd, lifting me toward the ceiling on a giant invisible wave of energy. Molly was bouncing up and down cheering; my parents were beaming with pride, and Evangeline's scowl had magically transformed into the tiniest of smirks. Even my boss looked moderately happy, and that was saying a lot for her.

My strength and determination were renewed as I lifted the card to read the introduction. I didn't get a chance to scan it before I felt everyone's eyes drilling into me expectantly. I was forced to just go for it: "We're thrilled to introduce the man of the hour, who will be sharing with you, in his own words, how much libraries have always meant to him and how they are a cornerstone of our democracy. And now, the Man, the Myth, the Legend: William R. 'Bull' Steyer!"

Wow, was it just me, or was that introduction just a little bit over-the-top? If I thought the room exploded in applause for my first spiel, the introduction blew the roof off the building. Fortunately, the waving, smiling mayor, who was several inches shorter than his wife in her skyscraper heels, raced up to the podium and snatched the microphone out of my hand so fast, he nearly knocked me over. I was thrilled to slink back into the crowd as he began to drone on and on about all the books he had ever read in his entire life.

I whipped out my camera and began taking pictures for Anna Cooper, my favorite patron, and the rest of the folks who followed the library on social media. Running our social media pages was another of my responsibilities. I didn't mind it, and it could be fun at times. It was yet another way I strived to make myself indispensable—and if we didn't collect enough money tonight, maybe it would be enough for me to keep my job.

THREE

After the mayor's impassioned plea for donations to the library, my fellow committee members and I went around collecting cash and checks in little metal pails, which we locked in the workroom behind the circulation desk to count after dinner.

"You've done such a great job with this event!" my mother said. Molly and Evangeline had gotten up to "mingle" (though I could hardly imagine Evangeline doing anything of the sort), and my parents snatched up their seats. Their table had been served first, so they'd eaten eons ago now. I was still finishing up.

"Thank you guys for coming." After recovering from my brush with death, *I mean public speaking*, my appetite returned full force, and I was able to stuff my face with the delicious catered meal.

"So that dark-haired girl you and Molly are hanging out with...that's Evangeline?" My mother glanced around, seemingly to make sure she wasn't coming back for her seat.

"Yeah, oh, sorry, I should have properly introduced you. I forgot you'd never met her in person before. She's our cataloguer..."

"What does that mean, exactly?" my dad jumped into the conversation.

"She catalogs books," I answered, which was met with blank stares from both of my parents, like I was speaking a different language. "So, librarians have to classify the books, right? So they can get shelved by subject and author?"

Now they nodded.

"So you can search for books in the library catalog," I went on, "and that's only possible because a cataloguer has documented all the metadata for each book."

Nope, I'd lost them again. *Oh, well.*

"She seems...different," my mother observed.

Evangeline was quiet and introverted, but we'd gotten to know each other well through the years. "She *is* different," I agreed, "but she's nice, I promise."

"Okay," my mom relented, but I could tell she was still a little uneasy about my friend. I was forty-two years old, and my mother was still concerned about the friends I was hanging out with.

"Did you get enough to eat?" I asked her and my father, and this time they nodded vigorously. *Subject changes for the win!*

My father rubbed his stomach with a satisfied grin on his face. "It was pretty darn good, too, wasn't it, Nancy?"

"The chicken was a little dry," my mother countered.

Oh no. This could be the start of another one of their infamous arguments.

Fortunately, I was saved when one of my colleagues put a hand on my shoulder. I turned my head to find Jada Booker looking down at me. "Hey, Sunshine."

"Hey, Jada, what's up?" She and Evangeline hung out from time to time since they were both part of tech services, but I hadn't really gotten a chance to know her yet. She was younger, probably in her early thirties, fresh out of library school, and this was her first job in management.

"Um, the mayor's wife is looking for you?" She shrugged like she didn't appreciate being forced to play messenger.

"Camille?" I looked around the room but didn't see the statuesque blonde anywhere.

"She said it's time to count the donations so her husband can announce the total," Jada reported.

"Oh, okay. Thanks for letting me know."

"Sure, whatever." She rolled her eyes and walked away on four-inch heels that complemented her sleek, form-fitting fuchsia dress. *Ah to be young and able to walk gracefully in heels again!* Though I wasn't sure there'd ever been a time in my life that I could have been called "graceful."

I turned to my parents. "Well, guess I gotta go."

"We'll see you later, honey." My mom covered my hand with hers and gave me a pat.

"Hope you've got a million bucks sitting down there!" my dad said, his bushy gray eyebrows waggling as he grinned at me.

"Million bucks? That'd be nice, but it would take us all night to count!" I joked, pulling my chair out. When I got to the doorway, I glanced back at the room, taking in all the townsfolk mingling and enjoying themselves at the party I planned. Did this group look like they'd just dropped a bunch of money to support the library? I couldn't tell, but I sure hoped so.

Soon, Susan would usher them all back downstairs for another performance from the magician and then dancing. I'd asked Molly to take some photos for me so I could post them on our social media. Then we'd give the mayor the final tally, and we'd all celebrate the library's good fortune—and my job being safe.

Minutes later, I was tucked away in the workroom behind the circulation desk tallying up the spoils while everyone else partied it up on the first floor, where the DJ was spinning oldies like records never went out of style. I was a little sad that I was missing all the elder townspeople's dance moves—always the best part of the night, but I was also anxious to see what kind of moolah we'd been able to rake in.

We'd been at it for about thirty minutes when the mayor's wife poked her head back in the room. "Well, what's the final count?"

I noticed she, Rosita and Heather had neglected their counting duties in favor of dancing. It spawned another trip down memory lane, back to high school, where I always ended up doing the work for group projects all by myself. At least I had the other committee members there to help me this time—and the mayor's wife's absence, as well as that of her clique, was painfully obvious to them as well.

Trying not to dwell on it, I gathered the piles of bills and checks counted by Harriett, Chris, Clara, Melanie, Daniel and Fred. They'd each slapped a bright pink Post-It note with the total of the pile on top. I began adding everything up on a calculator that was probably older than me. I wasn't sure I could trust its math, to be honest, any more than I trusted math that came out of my own calculator (i.e. my brain.)

When I did finally arrive at a number, I must have been wearing quite a look of shock because Melanie Cho exclaimed, "I can't tell if your expression is a good sign or a bad sign, Sunshine!"

"Uh, I think it's good? Hold on a sec..." I hastily re-added all the numbers again and arrived at the very same result. My heart pounded, thudding against my ribs as I realized that the total far exceeded my expectations.

If this figure was accurate, we'd just pulled off the most successful gala in the history of the library. It was my first time at the helm, and I managed to achieve results far beyond anyone else's. I kept looking down at the calculator to make sure the number hadn't changed. Nope, it remained the same. As waves of joy crashed over me, I sent up prayers of gratitude for making our event so successful.

"Well, don't hold us in suspense," Camille snarked, flanked by her clique in their sparkly, too-tight gowns.

"It's actually...wow..." I shook my head, still trying to get past my shock and wrap my head around the figure displayed on the calculator. "Including the donations that were collected before the event, we raised nearly a hundred thousand dollars," I gasped.

Everyone was silent for a moment, their jaws hanging open in awe. Then Camille's face scrunched up. "A hundred thousand?" She looked at her friends and then planted her suspicious glare right on me. "The most we've ever raised in an evening is seventy-two. A hundred can't be right. Let's recount."

"I already added it up twice, and we don't have time to do it again," I argued. "Susan and the mayor are expecting me to give them the figure before ten o'clock so they can announce our final count before everyone goes home. It's 9:50 right now."

"There was a particularly large donation from Willa Bryce Monroe in my pile," committee member Fred Hillary pointed out. "Very substantial, actually."

I'd never been privy to the actual checks as they were received from donors, so I didn't know what the usual amounts were, but Mrs. Monroe was the wealthiest person in Bryce Beach. A widow, she lived on a property listed in the National Register of Historic Places, and she had traced her ancestry all the way back to town founder Nathaniel Bryce. I had to admit, my eyes bugged out a little when I saw the size of her donation. It was far bigger than anyone else's.

Camille rolled her eyes at her friends, then turned her focus to me. "Fine, you better hurry up and get out there. But let me go out first. Bull won't want to announce my total until I'm by his side."

My total? I fought very hard not to roll my own eyes at her dramatic insinuation that a) the donations were hers and b) the mayor needed her beside him to announce the results of *the committee's* fundraising efforts, even if she was the chairwoman. I succeeded in my attempt by the skin of my teeth, then followed the trio out of the room, the final tally written on a pink Post-It note I stuck to my index finger.

Most of the party-goers were still mulling about the makeshift dance floor, but the energy levels had significantly waned now that the evening was nearly over. I saw Susan talking to Tom, Barbara, Jada and Evangeline across the room, so I headed over to join them, giving Camille ample time to take her place next to the mayor. Besides, I was excited to share the news with my colleagues of how much money we'd brought in.

I didn't even realize how much relief that huge number brought me until I glanced back down at it. We received a number of grants and some state and city funds, but we hadn't received enough money for raises or to increase our budgets for collections for a year or two now. And it always seemed to be the YA collection that suffered the most.

I was petrified that if our gala didn't go well, and Susan was forced to let a staff member go, it would be me. Their potential arguments rang in my ears: *Teens don't need the public library! They have plenty of other places to hang out. They have a library at their school. They hardly even come in here.*

It was true that our youth patronage had gone down in the past year, but most of it was because I'd lost my programming budget, not to mention half my budget for buying new books and magazines. With this chunk of money, I'd have a little to play with, and I could start luring the teens of Bryce Beach back into the library in no time!

"What do you have, Baker?" Susan called me by my last name.

My eyes narrowed, unable to understand why people did that. Being called by my first name was bad enough, but it was intolerable to be called by my last name. I ignored that and focused on the pink Post-It, waving it toward her. "I think you're gonna like this figure!"

Her eyes lit up when she peeled it off my finger and absorbed the number. Her eyes never lit up. She was truly impressed. I was *so* getting a raise!

"I've gotta go make sure the activities room gets cleaned up," she said. "Why don't you take this over to the mayor? He might even let *you* make the announcement."

"Me?" I stood there, frozen in place.

"Yes, you did a good job with the welcome and mayor's introduction. And you pulled off a very successful event." She patted me on the shoulder. "Congratulations."

My boss had never praised me. Ever. If I was shocked over the figure we'd collected, this was even more momentous. I watched her head up the stairs to the second level, my comfy flats still glued to the floor.

Molly and Evangeline were at my sides in a flash. "What just happened? How did we do?" they both talked over each other.

Camille was giving me the stink-eye. "I have to get this over to my husband so he can announce it."

They both kept asking me questions, but I waved them off. There'd be plenty of time to celebrate after we let everyone know how much we'd raised.

Now with laser focus, I marched those comfy flats over to where Mayor Steyer and Camille were standing, schmoozing with Willa Bryce Monroe and a few other swanky townsfolk. "We have our final number," I interrupted their conversation.

"I already told him," Camile said, turning to me with a smug smile.

I ignored her and directed my attention solely to the mayor. "It's time to make the announcement. Do you want me to do it, or would you prefer—"

"I'll do it!" Bull Steyer exclaimed, standing up straight and adjusting his tie. "C'mon!" He looked down at me with a grin that told me to follow him to the DJ booth. Camille huffed out something that I didn't hear, then I saw her whisper to her two besties before she slipped down the hall.

Where is she going? I wondered as the music faded out and Mayor Steyer took the microphone from the DJ. The crowd started to quiet down and turn their attention to the DJ booth.

I thought Miss Important had to be by her husband's side as he read off the figure?

The mayor announced, "We have our final figure for tonight's donations. Before I tell you the amount we raised, I just want to reiterate how important the library is to our community and remind you of all the vital work that goes on within these walls. Our town is lucky to have such a great library staff and leadership, and everyone who worked really hard to pull off tonight's event."

The crowd applauded, even though he hadn't given the number yet. *Talk about* Great Expectations!

My parents flashed me a look that said, "We're proud of you no matter how much it is!"

Willa Bryce Monroe wore a happy grin as if she had a good idea her donation had rocketed us to a never-before-achieved amount.

"Ninety-nine thousand, nine hundred and fifty-two dollars!" the mayor announced, and the crowd erupted in applause, cheers, and general merriment. For an older crowd who was likely nearing their bedtimes, the noise they generated was pretty impressive.

"Well, golly, I'll chip in the other forty-eight bucks myself to make it an even one hundred grand!" Mayor Steyer continued as the DJ struck up "Celebration" by Kool & the Gang.

Everyone was smiling, joy blossoming on their elated faces as they exchanged hugs and high-fives and rather exuberant whoops and hollers. And then...

The sound of a door slamming shut and glass shattering brought all the chaos to an immediate halt.

The entire crowd moved from the makeshift dance floor set up in the reference and reading area to check out what had happened. I was at the back of the pack, but as soon as I saw the source of the shattering sound, a bolt of panic ripped through me.

The Founders' Bible, the most priceless relic in Bryce Beach, given to the library upon the dedication of the building in the 1950s, was gone. The glass case where it was on display for decades had been smashed to smithereens, and broken glass glittered like diamonds all over the floor.

My first instinct was to look around for Susan. She would know what to do. Then I remembered she'd gone to the activities room upstairs where they'd served dinner to supervise the cleanup.

My head swiveled toward the mayor, who was animatedly talking on his cell phone. Evangeline and Molly appeared beside me moments later.

"Oh my gosh! Did anyone see what happened?" Molly asked, looking around.

Our gala guests had found their voices, and a panicked chatter was welling up among the crowd like a distant siren growing closer and closer. The mayor slid his phone into his pocket and used his fingers to produce a shrill, ear-piercing whistle, instantly quieting everyone gathered around the broken display case that had held the now missing artifact.

"The Bryce Beach PD is on their way," he said. "No one goes anywhere."

That was when I remembered that the mayor's wife had disappeared right before his speech. I turned to my friends. "Did anyone see where Camille went right before the figure was announced?"

Molly's eyebrows quirked as she pressed her lips together thoughtfully. Jada shook her head and looked down at the floor.

Evangeline shrugged. "I thought I saw her head down the hall toward the offices. Maybe to the restroom?"

There was a staff restroom down the hallway to the

right of the circulation desk. But also down that hallway was a back entrance to the office area that could otherwise only be accessed through the gate at the circulation counter. My heart started to flutter in my chest as a sudden worry about the donations cycled through me—the money was in the workroom in that office area, and no one was guarding it.

"Come on," I said to my friends. "Follow me." As stealthily as possible, I wormed my way through the dumbfounded crowd, who had already started to chatter again amongst themselves. My two colleagues were hot on my heels.

We lifted the gate to the circulation desk and slipped into the staff-only area, weaving around some bookshelves where we kept holds for patrons and staged returned books for shelving. I used my key to unlock the offices, then made my way back to the workroom, where we'd counted the money. We'd left all the cash in one metal pail and the checks in another.

As soon as I turned on the light, my worst nightmare came to life:

Both pails were sitting on the counter, completely empty.

FOUR

The next day, Sunday, I went to church.

I was exhausted by the events of Saturday night, and I'd replayed the scenes of what transpired at the gala in my head a million times. Talk about the highest of highs and the lowest of lows. Last night was a roller coaster, and now the ride still wasn't over. In some ways, it seemed like it was just beginning because we had no idea what happened. The puzzle pieces were scattered just like the glass all over the lobby floor from the Founders' Bible display case. Right now I didn't know if those pieces would ever come together to give us a clear picture of who stole the future of the Bryce Beach Public Library.

My dad wore a somber face as he greeted me in the church parking lot. "You doing okay, Sunny?" He was the only one allowed to call me that.

"I just don't know where I went wrong…" My voice trailed off when I realized my mom wasn't with him. "Where's Mom?"

He shook his head. "She was so upset last night, so worried about you, she couldn't sleep. She was up all night, so she decided to stay home today."

As horrible as I felt, I felt even more horrible that my mother was suffering right alongside me. She was such a sensitive, empathetic soul. Maybe I could take her lunch after the service. "Oh, great. Now I feel even worse."

My dad, who was tall and strong, even if he was shrinking a bit with age, wrapped his arms around me and pulled me to his chest. "It'll be okay, Sunny. Everything will work out; you'll see."

"I wish I could believe that." I smoothed down my boring gray dress I'd chosen because it matched my mood and walked with him inside the building, where we greeted other members of the congregation before settling into our family's pew.

By now, I was sure everyone had heard what happened at the gala, even the people who weren't in attendance. Small towns were excellent at spreading the word about everything from thefts of priceless relics to who's getting married to who's having the next garage sale. Fortunately, my fellow churchgoers seemed to understand I needed space because no one approached me. I must have had a shell-shocked look on my face that warned them to stay away.

As I was trying to settle my mind into a state conducive to worship, I remembered our pastor had retired last month, and no one had been hired to take his place. Pastor Marks was our minister for as long as I could remember, and no one would be able to fill his shoes. Just thinking about that—and having to sit through a sermon delivered by someone who wasn't Pastor Marks —made me even sadder.

After the prayer, a few hymns, and a special performance of "How Great Thou Art" by a tenor with a rather *tremolo* voice, the guest minister took the pulpit and started off by telling a story. I struggled to stay engaged and not let my mind wander.

How was I going to face my boss tomorrow morning?

I felt like this was all my fault. I should have put the donations someplace safer than the workroom. I should have thought to have them record all the checks as they were counting—but we were in such a big hurry to get the tally!

I thought the doors were all locked, but I wasn't the last one out—I had to take the Post-It note to the mayor, and the rest of the committee followed me out of the room. If someone left the door open...

Then I found myself running through the sequence of events from the time we heard the glass break until I finally left the library and went home. Officer Harmon from the Bryce Beach Police Department arrived only five minutes after the mayor called him. He and his partner, a young female cadet named Allison Adams, set about taking statements from the key witnesses and collecting names and telephone numbers of everyone else. There were still at least fifty people in the building when the mayor announced the sum of the donations.

I found my boss upstairs in the activities room. She was helping the catering staff clear away dishes and tablecloths from the dinner. The caterers had music playing to make their work faster and more enjoyable, and it was immediately apparent that none of them heard the commotion on the first floor.

So I had to be the one to deliver the bad news to my boss.

Susan Gooch, who was one of the most pragmatic and even-tempered people I'd ever met, nearly crumbled to the floor in shock and despair. I caught her, and she threw her arms around me, sobbing.

I still felt her arms around my shoulders now—this version of my boss was the polar opposite of the stoic woman who ruled the library with an iron fist. But Susan knew what was at stake if we didn't recover the stolen funds and the Founders' Bible. The latter was irreplaceable; it was as simple as that. But the funds were the only way we'd be able to keep the doors to the library open all year, increase our collections, and maintain our current staffing levels.

And I still heard her voice echo in my ears every time I recalled her look of devastation. "Sunshine," she'd said, "I want you to work with the police on this investigation. You were the staff member in charge of the gala, and you are the one who saw all the checks that came in. You've already been meeting with the Friends of the Library for the last six months to plan this event, so it will be easy for you to coordinate with them if the police need to question anyone further."

That was all true, but... Well, actually, I hadn't seen all of the checks. And we didn't have time to document all of them before they were stolen, so we weren't sure how many they were or who wrote them. I'm clearly not fit to be in charge of anything!

"Are you sure it wouldn't be better if you were in charge?" I hadn't wanted to overstep my bounds, but I was feeling terribly unqualified to represent the whole library on this matter of utmost importance. Our jobs were at stake! The future of the community's access to information, literature, and programming was at stake!

Planning an event was one thing, but being responsible for the investigation? Plus, I had already screwed up the event. How could I be trusted to see this through?

"I have faith in you, Sunshine," she told me. When I looked at her in the harsh lighting of the activities room, it looked like she'd aged a decade just since dinner. "Bring back our money and our Bible."

M onday morning, I trudged into work carrying this heavy burden on my shoulders. My first task would be to call the Bryce Beach PD and see where they were in their investigation. Then I would go from there.

"Hey, you're popular today," Molly said as I came in the back door of the library, winding my way through the storage room that connected to the technical services workspace. I wasn't expecting Molly to ambush me, so my heart nearly leapt out of my ribcage.

Evangeline offered up a little wave from her cataloguing hidey-hole. "Recovered from the big gala?"

Molly and I stopped at her office door. "Recovered?" I shook my head. "Until that money is recovered, I won't be able to either."

"The Chief of Police is here to talk to her about it, in fact," Molly added.

"What?!" I looked at her incredulously. "Why didn't you tell me?"

The Chief of Police? Ack! I was expecting Officer Harmon and his sidekick Cadet Adams from Saturday night.

"I said, 'You're popular around here,'" Molly repeated, rolling her eyes and lifting one shoulder in a shrug.

I spouted off a breathy huff and left the two of them standing there so I could track down the chief and not make him wait any longer than necessary. Weaving my way through the library, memories bombarded me from Saturday night's trip along that same path. When I reached the front of the circulation desk, I walked toward the periodical area, where the Chief of Police sat on a bench reading the most current edition of *The Bryce Beach Gazette*, which we always displayed on a newspaper stick.

One glance toward the lobby revealed that the display case where the Founders' Bible had been kept for decades was gone. All the glass had been swept up. There was just a big empty space in the middle of the floor where it had once stood, only marked by the spotlight shining down from the chandelier suspended above it.

"Chief James?"

My voice caused his head to bob up from the newspaper, then his dark brown eyes met mine. He was a tall hulk of a man, easily six feet four, with massive arms and a thick neck. He stood up, set the newspaper stick down on the bench and extended his hand.

"Hi, I'm Sunshine Baker, Young Adult Librarian," I introduced myself.

I reached out to shake, feeling his warmth seep into my skin as my hand was dwarfed in his. His grip was firm, but the contact was brief, and when he pulled away, he straightened to his full height and nodded, the little curl of a smile that had been on his lips when he first greeted me fading as the seriousness of the situation rose up like giant walls around us.

He scrubbed his hand over his bald brown head as he peered down at me, making me feel as small as a child. "Is there a place we can talk about the events of Saturday night?"

"Sure, let's go up to the activities room. There won't be anyone up there this early in the morning."

The library had just opened, and the only patrons were the little elderly couple who lived next door. They came over to read the newspaper first thing every morning. On Mondays, they browsed the stacks, and each picked out two books. As we made our way to the activities room, I spotted them on the second floor in the midst of their Monday routine.

I gestured to a chair near the podium where I'd made my speech on Saturday night. The large square tables had been moved back into place, replacing the round ones used for the gala. Chief James took a seat at one of the tables, and I sat across from him, folding my hands together on the surface. I needed a notepad or a file folder. I felt practically naked sitting there with his dark, inquisitive eyes on me. He had the type of eyes that never missed a thing—just the type you'd expect someone in law enforcement to have.

"I've been reading through the report Officer Harmon wrote up." Chief James glanced down at what appeared to be the report in question. "There's not a lot to go on, and there haven't been any fingerprints recovered from either the display case where the Bible was stolen or from the workroom where the donations were stolen."

"I'm sorry to hear that." As soon as the words came out of my mouth, I wanted to smack myself silly. My statement sounded so flippant. There was no denying this man made me nervous, and I hadn't done anything wrong!

The chief pursed his lips as he tapped his pen against the manila file folder. "That means gloves were used. The whole thing was most likely premeditated."

"So someone who was at the gala had planned to steal the Bible and the money all along?" I questioned. "The same person did both?"

"The two thefts happened in such close proximity, I'd venture the perpetrators were in cahoots." The "P's" of "perpetrators" popped off the chief's lips as he stabbed his dark stare into me.

"You think there was more than one suspect?" I had to admit, I was tapping into my inner Nancy Drew at this point.

"It's possible someone acted alone, but we need to do some further investigation."

"I can't believe someone actually infiltrated our gala."

I shook my head, stunned by the notion. I'd seen the guest list. I knew every single name on it—if not in person, I'd at least heard of each guest before. "Do you think their target was the Bible, and then they decided to go for the money too, or...?"

"I'm not going to discuss the particulars of the investigation with you, Miss Baker. But I did want to ask you some questions."

"Alright." His brusque tone sent a pang of disappointment through me.

He flipped through a few full pages of his spiralbound notebook until he reached a blank page, then he poised his pen over the paper. "Where were you when the Bible was stolen?"

Wait. Was I a suspect?

"Chief James, I assure you, I had nothing to do with either theft. I organized the event. I love my library and my town. I would never do anything to hurt either one of them," I said, not able to keep the defensiveness out of my tone.

"I just need you to answer the question, Miss Baker." His eyes narrowed slightly. "Is it Miss?"

I nodded. "Or Ms."

I waited for him to say something further but then realized he was still waiting for me to answer his question. "I was standing not far from the mayor when he announced the sum of our donations. He was reading the figure off a pink Post-It note I had written the total on and handed to him only a minute or two before the announcement."

Chief James scribbled a few lines on the notepad.

"And you were the one who discovered the money was missing?"

I nodded. "The glass shattered in the lobby, and everyone moved that way to see what happened. I followed. Once we figured out it was the Bible, I felt compelled to check on the donations."

"And were the doors to the office area locked?" he questioned.

"They were from the circulation desk entrance," I said. "I didn't check the back door...the one by the restroom."

That was when I remembered the mayor's wife heading down the hallway right before her husband made the announcement. Molly and Evangeline had theorized she'd gone to use the staff restroom, but she could have snuck into the offices through the back door if it was unlocked. She didn't have a key.

What about the Bible, though?

Well, I didn't see Rosita or Heather during the announcement. What if they bashed in the display case and stole the Bible to create a distraction so Camille could steal the money?

"Either way...locked or unlocked...who knew the donations were being kept in that workroom?"

I had thought of that. "Just the Friends of the Library committee, I think...and a few library employees."

Oh. So I see how that looks.

"You don't think one of us stole the money we worked so hard to raise, do you?" Again I felt like I was being accused, and I didn't like it one bit. Where was the motive?

The chief tilted his head a little but didn't say a word, just finished writing down a few things before looking at me again. "I'm going to need a list of everyone who had access to that workroom, including committee members and librarians with keys. Include those who were in attendance at the gala, and any who were not. There's a back entrance to the building, correct? An entrance anyone with a key could access?" He handed me a card as I nodded. "Email me the list as soon as you can, and include contact information. In the meantime, I'll be interviewing other staff."

He stood up and gathered his notepad and manila folder. "Oh, one more thing: do you have a list of the donors who wrote checks?"

I shook my head. "We didn't get a chance to document all of them. We were in such a hurry to get the total number. Why, could we stop payment on them if we had a list?"

He smirked. "We could, but I'd rather see if the checks are cashed and by whom. You'll need to submit a list of all attendees as well as the other information I asked for. We'll have to ask donors to monitor their bank accounts so we know where the checks were deposited, if anyone does attempt to deposit them. Maybe they planned to just pocket the cash."

I swallowed a lungful of air and nodded. "Anything else?"

"I'll be in touch if I have further questions."

After watching him leave, his burly figure lumbering out of the building, I stood there for a moment in shock.

He sounded like he thought one of us was responsible for stealing the gala funds.

One of us!

The very people the funds were going to help.

I t was a warm spring day, and Molly, Evangeline and I decided to eat our lunches in the library's courtyard. It was accessible on the other side of the reading room, and we often did children's programming out there when the weather was nice. A crisp breeze was blowing in off the water, which was only a few blocks from the library, and the tree branches, whose spring leaves were finally unfurling, were waving in the air as wispy clouds floated past on their journey to the ocean.

"What did you think of Chief James?" Molly asked, her pale blue eyes darting between Evangeline and me.

Evangeline set down her fork in her salad bowl. "Seems like a pretty straightforward guy."

"He thinks one of us did it, you know," I said, unable to contain my instant dislike of the man.

"You think so? His questions seemed unbiased to me," Evangeline insisted. "He asked, what did we see? When did we see it?"

"He wants me to provide a list of everyone who has access to that workroom where we were keeping the funds during the gala," I shared.

"That seems pretty standard," Molly argued.

"Oh, so you're all on his side!" I refused to believe

someone on our committee or library staff stole the money.

"Hey, I have to tell you something," Evangeline interrupted the tirade I was about to embark upon against the chief accusing one of us of sabotaging our own library.

"What?" Molly popped a grape into her mouth, then gave our dark-haired friend her attention.

Evangeline leaned in, then glanced around to make sure no one was watching or listening. We were outside. Alone. There might have been a few birds or a squirrel, but definitely no humans. "Remember how we saw Camille Steyer heading down the hallway toward the offices right before the donation total was announced?"

"Yeah?" I'd thought that was suspicious too.

"Well," our cataloguer friend continued, seeming to enjoy holding us in suspense, "I overheard her and her little Mean Girl clique talking about the library and her husband on Saturday night."

"You did?!" I was shocked I was just now hearing this. My friend was holding out on me?! "What did they say?"

"I didn't want to repeat it because I was technically eavesdropping, and repeating it is just spreading gossip, but..." She looked around to make sure no humans had magically appeared since her last surveillance. Nope, still just birds. "But maybe it's relevant to the case?"

"What did she say, E?" Molly asked, bouncing up and down on the bench like she could barely contain herself for one more second.

"She said something about how she was sick of her husband's job and having to support stupid causes like the library, and she really hoped he didn't get elected for another term."

My hand flew to my mouth, covering up my gasp. "Wow, she really said that?"

Evangeline nodded. "Yup. I always thought she and her husband were so smarmy, but now, seeing how she really feels about the library..."

"Then why is she on the Friends of the Library committee? She's the committee chair, for crying out loud!" Molly exclaimed. "I mean, if she thinks the library is stupid and is a stupid cause, why actually volunteer to help the library?"

"Maybe Bull put her up to it," Evangeline hypothesized. "Because it makes her look like she cares about the community, which makes him look good. And if she chaired the committee that raised a lot of money for the library, then that might help him get elected."

"But what if she's trying to sabotage his election?" I played devil's advocate. "What if she was only on the committee to steal the money and make him and the library look bad?"

Molly laughed, throwing her head back as a loud, piercing giggle spilled out. They probably heard her clear down at the beach. "You guys," she said in between snorts, "all your conspiracy theories. So funny!"

"Well, who do you think did it, Molls?" I fired back at her. If we were so funny with our wild conspiracy theories, surely she had a better idea who our prime suspect should be.

She shrugged. "Fortunately, it's not a crime I have to solve. It's the police's job to figure it out."

I cleared my throat. "If that money isn't recovered and put into the library's bank account... Well, I don't have to tell you that we're going to have a budget crisis. One of us will get fired. I guarantee it."

The color drained from my friend's already pale face. She sucked in a breath and gathered her long blonde hair into her fist, arranging it over her shoulder like she always did when she was nervous. "I'm sure it won't come down to that. And I'm sure the police will recover the money. Especially if it *is* an inside job—should be easy to figure out, right?"

"What about the Founders' Bible?" Evangeline's eyebrows arched as she went back to nibbling on her salad, her long nose wiggling like a rabbit's as she chewed. "Why did they take it?"

"What would be Camille's motive to take the Bible?" Molly asked. Her face was so pinched, it was hard to believe she was laughing her head off mere moments ago.

I took a deep breath, putting all the puzzle pieces together. "If she wants to sabotage her husband's re-election campaign...what better way than to steal our town's most precious artifact right under his nose?"

I had my very first lead on my very first case. Nancy Drew, eat your heart out!

FIVE

"You wanted to see me?" I pushed the door to my boss's office open just far enough to meet her gaze.

"Yes, Sunshine, come in." She worked up a forced smile and gestured to the chair across from her. Then she hovered her cursor over the X on the browser window she had open.

I only caught a brief glimpse of the window before the screen returned to her desktop background, which was a photo of her black Labrador retriever, Bart. The screen she'd been looking at was a beach, but not Bryce Beach. The water was crystal clear as it rolled onto white sand and a bright teal as it stretched toward the horizon. Palm trees waved their long green fronds over the surf. It looked like a tropical paradise. *Sigh.* I loved living in Bryce Beach, but it wasn't *that* type of beach.

"Planning a vacation?" I asked her, thinking it might elicit a real smile.

Instead, the corners of her lips turned down. "Did you talk to Chief James today?"

"Yes, sure did. I believe he made the rounds interviewing everyone."

"I must have been at lunch when he stopped by my office," she sighed. "Did you learn anything?"

Revealing my theories to Susan about the mayor's wife or how Chief James implied one of the library staff was the perpetrator seemed like a bad idea, so I kept my mouth shut—not the easiest feat for me.

"Not much. He seemed to be asking standard questions, like who had access to the workroom."

Susan ran her fingers through her short gray hair. "I just don't understand why someone would take that Bible." She shook her head as she stared down at her desk, presumably looking for answers. "The money, I get it. Though most of it was in checks, and it's not like they'll be able to cash them. The Bible? It has no market value. Where are they going to sell a four-hundred-year-old falling-apart Bible?"

"Right," I agreed. "It's almost like the person who did it doesn't want the money. They only want to hurt the library."

"That's what I've been thinking about." She nodded slowly, her mind still wrapping itself around all the unanswered questions. I'd never seen my boss so fragile or emotional. She had a backbone of steel and ice water running through her veins. This whole...heist, for lack of a better term...had just demolished her. It was painful to see her crumble like this. "It makes no sense to me how someone could be so cruel..."

It actually made sense to me...if Camille Steyer was to blame. She wouldn't care about the money. She only wanted to hurt the library and her husband's chances of re-election.

"Sunshine," my boss leaned toward me, her fingers interlaced on her desk, "you have to find out what happened. I don't think the police are going to get anywhere, and if they don't get a lead soon, they're not even going to pursue it. Whether we get the money back or the Bible isn't that important to *them*. But it's vital to *us*."

"I can try to poke around," I agreed, downplaying my investment. I was already very much into this whole Nancy Drew thing I had going on.

"I'm afraid of what might happen if we don't recover that money..." She sucked in a breath and shook her head, her eyes full of concern. "We might not survive..."

❦

My parents had invited me over for dinner, but I suspected it was more to get the scoop on the case than it was because they wanted to see me. When I arrived, I learned they'd also invited my brother, River, who had his full entourage of my sister-in-law, Isabelle, and their twin sons, Jacob and Andrew, with him.

The house was in full chaos mode as soon as I stepped through the door. So much for a peaceful respite after work. My head was already starting to pound, and I was longing for the solitude of my own place and my kitties, but my mother wrapped her arms around my waist and planted a huge kiss on my cheek.

"You looked so beautiful at the gala," she said. "Why don't you wear your hair like that more often?"

I looked at her, completely flummoxed as to what she was talking about. "I wore my hair the same way I always do." It was thick and naturally curly. There wasn't a lot I could do with it.

"It looked fuller," she insisted. "Bouncier."

I shook off that weird comment and turned to my father, who also pulled me in for a hug. "Hey, Sunny Bunny."

I tried not to roll my eyes at my childhood nickname. My father was the only one I allowed to call me "Sunny," and anyone else who dared to call me "Sunny Bunny" would probably never live to call me that a second time.

Wow, I am in full snark mode tonight, I thought, wincing at my own internal dialogue. I'd been praying for God to give me more patience and less attitude, but it looked like I needed to double up my efforts.

"Hey, River, Izzy." I dipped my chin in acknowledgment of my brother and sister-in-law, who were already seated at my parents' dining room table. "Where are the boys?"

"They're in the family room playing," Isabelle sighed, sounding as if she hoped maybe they'd entertain themselves for a while. The two eight-year-olds were a handful, but they were my buds. I figured I'd better go say hello so they didn't think their Aunt Sunshine didn't love them anymore.

As I headed into the family room, my mother called out my name, "Sunshine? Where are you going?"

"To see Jake and Drew." I narrowly avoided adding "duh" to the end of my statement. *See?* My prayers were working.

"Oh no you're not," my mom said. "You're going to sit down at this table and tell us what is going on at the library before the boys come in for dinner!"

I whipped around and saw four pairs of eyes drilling into me, full of suspense and intrigue. Not seeing any way out of the situation, I plopped myself down in one of the oak chairs and huffed out a deep groan.

"Don't want the boys to know there's a criminal running amok in Bryce Beach?" I questioned, waggling my eyebrows up and down.

"Come on, sweetheart. Isn't everyone in the library up in arms?" my dad asked.

"Up in arms? We're librarians," I countered, trying to keep the mood light. "We're pacifists. We only arm ourselves with books and information."

"Not everyone thinks they need a gun to protect themselves, Phil," my mom added.

A grunt and clenched jaw were my father's initial responses. And then: "First of all, 'up in arms' is an expression. And second of all, if someone would have been armed at the gala, maybe none of this would have happened!"

Oh no, here we go again. We hadn't even started the conversation, and they were already arguing their opposing political agendas. River and Izzy both shot me "the look," the one we were all aware of. It meant,

"Godspeed. Hope we make it out of this conversation alive."

I cleared my throat and prepared myself for battle—though it was hard to take up "arms" of information when it was in such short supply. "I don't know anything yet," was all I said.

"What did the police say?" my father asked.

"Did they find any fingerprints?" River questioned.

My mother shook her head. "I don't know if you're safe there, honey. What if the thief comes back? I've barely been able to sleep at night, I'm so worried about you!"

"Has anyone deposited the money?" Izzy asked. "Checked for the Founders' Bible on eBay?"

"I have some theories about what might have happened," I cut everyone off. In my family, I usually had to talk over everyone to be heard, but it was so quiet, you could have heard a pin drop after the word "theories" came out of my mouth.

"What kind of theories?" my brother finally asked.

"I can't disclose the details of an ongoing investigation," I said, trying to sound detached and professional, "but Chief James seems to think someone on our staff did it, and I refuse to believe any of us would sabotage the library like that." In the end, I wasn't really able to disguise my opinion of that nonsense.

My mother gasped, her hand flying up to cover her mouth. "He really thinks it was an inside job?"

"He didn't say that, exactly. But he did ask me for a list of everyone who has access to the workroom where the money was being kept when it was stolen."

"Chief James is a very smart man," my father interjected. "If anyone can get to the bottom of this, it's him."

I couldn't stop the scoff before it flew out of my mouth, along with perhaps a tiny droplet of spittle. *Oops.* I was less than impressed with Chief James. But I knew my dad was a big fan. He was a big fan of law and order, and since hardly anything ever happened in our little town, Chief James had created at least the illusion of law and order—until this.

"Did you meet him?" Izzy asked, her eyes growing wide. "He did a talk at the boys' school last year, and he was so interesting and articulate. They loved his stories!"

"Oh for Pete's sake." I scrubbed my hand down my face. "Why don't you guys just invite Chief James to dinner next time instead of me if you love the guy that much?"

"He's single, you know," my mother added.

My palm flew to my forehead as my headache instantly intensified. "Drew! Jake!" I yelled, sliding my chair back and rising from the table. I didn't need this conversation to go one word further.

Seconds later, I was up to my eyeballs in little boy hugs. Just like I liked it.

***

When I finally made it home that night, I thought I would fall asleep as soon as my head hit the pillow. I completed all my normal bedtime tasks: washing my face, brushing my teeth, putting on my pajamas, devouring a chapter or two of my latest read, and then saying my prayers. I climbed into bed, where Bond and Paige had already claimed their spots: Bond by my feet and Paige by my hip. But the longer I lay there, the more it felt like my heart was racing and my eyes were bugging out.

Scenes from the library gala kept playing over and over again in my head like I was watching a video that someone kept stopping, rewinding, and playing again. The glass of the Founders' Bible display case must have shattered in my memory a dozen or more times before I bolted upright in bed.

All I could think about was Camille's little cheerleader posse busting that glass to create a diversion so she could go back to the workroom and steal the proceeds from the gala. Camille was the type of person whom people loved to hate. It wasn't her fault she was beautiful, elegant, and svelte—and married to the mayor. She was seemingly perfect, but she didn't have a humble bone in her body. Sure, everyone was nice to her face, but behind her back, there was nothing but gossip and eyerolling.

If what Evangeline overheard was true, Camille loathed being the mayor's wife and thought the library was worthless. She pretended to be committed to the cause, even chairing our committee, but who was really doing all the work? Me—along with a few of the other committee members. Would she really stoop so low as to ruin all our hard work and put the library's future in jeopardy? Did she really think she could get away with stealing the library's money and absconding with our town's most precious relic?

She wasn't the least bit likable, but was she actually a duplicitous snake?

For all the questions I had, there was something I knew for certain deep down in my heart:

Chief James would never, ever suspect Camille Steyer of committing this crime. Bull and Camille Steyer were probably the first two people he crossed off his list of suspects.

So if I didn't stay on the case and get to the bottom of this...

1. I might lose my job,

and

2. Camille Steyer might get away with it!

I wasn't about to let that happen.

SIX

We were blessed with another nice day of weather, so my co-conspirators and I assumed our usual positions at the picnic table in the courtyard and pulled out our respective lunches. I had leftovers from dinner at my parents' last night, which my mother had lovingly packed in little Tupperware containers. I was sure that would garner a snarky comment from Evangeline, but they were delicious, so I didn't really care what she thought. Molly had been on some weird rice and mushrooms diet, and her stir fry or whatever it was stunk to high heavens. At least mine smelled good. And tasted amazing!

"So, it occurred to me last night that if Camille Steyer is our culprit, then she's going to get away with it scot-free because Chief James would never, ever cross Mayor Steyer. He'd never even question them," I shared with my comrades.

Evangeline's eyes narrowed as she peeled her orange,

then popped a section into her mouth. She spit out a seed into her napkin before responding, "Do you think I should tell Chief James what I overheard?"

"Maybe. I want to get some more information first." I pulled out a notebook I'd been carrying around with me. I'd taken the liberty of writing down the names of everyone who was at the library gala on Saturday evening. And in true librarian fashion, I'd divided them into categories: Friends of the Library Committee Members, Library Staff, and Townsfolk. Then the names were alphabetized. Naturally.

"Ooooh, is that what I think it is?" Molly's eyes trailed over the names when I flipped the cover over, revealing the first page of my flowing script.

"Yep. Everyone at the gala." I tapped my pencil against the lined paper. "Anyone we can cross off as suspects?"

"Um, all of us?" Evangeline suggested, her lips curling into a tiny smirk before she sucked another orange slice into her mouth.

"Right! We didn't do it!" Molly giggled.

That was true. I drew lines through each of our names. "Who else?"

"Well, I'm sure Chief James's parents didn't do it," Evangeline said. "Or your parents either, for that matter."

Molly was still laughing from earlier, but her chuckles peaked again before dying down. "The most adorable couple on earth? Nope, they've gotta be innocent, or my faith in humankind will be destroyed forever!"

"And the Wilsons, that sweet little couple who goes to our church," I added, ignoring Molly's remark. "I'm sure they're beyond reproach. Plus she's in a wheelchair, and he walks with a cane."

"Willa Bryce Monroe?" Molly's eyebrow rose. "She always donates a lot, right? Why would she steal the money?"

"True. I saw her check, guys. It was twenty grand—about twenty percent of what we collected." I probably shouldn't have disclosed the amount, but I could trust my two best friends, right?

Molly's mouth formed an O. "I can't imagine having so much money that I could give away twenty thousand."

Evangeline sipped from her water bottle before nodding. "Must be nice."

"Well, she was born into money, then she married rich. At least she's generous!" I crossed her off the list and stopped at the next few names. They were townspeople I didn't know very well.

"They're all rich too. Old money," Evangeline said. "Doubtful any of them were involved."

We made it through all the citizens of Bryce Beach who weren't connected to the library or the Friends of the Library. These were the people who came to the gala to show their support for the library and donate money to the cause. There were a few names no one could vouch for, so we left them on the list before moving on to the Friends of the Library committee.

"I don't know why anyone would bust their behinds working on a committee year after year—most of these members have been involved with the Friends of the Library for a long time, decades even—just to steal the proceeds of the biggest fundraising effort of the year." My gaze shifted between my two friends, awaiting their reaction.

"And to steal the Founders' Bible!" Molly added. "I can't believe anybody who cares about our town would have the nerve to do that."

"None of these members were new this year?" Evangeline questioned, grabbing the notebook to peruse the list of names. "What about Melanie Cho?"

"She's been involved for a year or two," I answered. "I don't know her well, but she's lovely. She owns the art gallery in town."

"I can't imagine a businessowner would want to jeopardize their reputation in this town," Molly remarked. "I mean, reputation is everything here." She paused and tilted her head. "Unless..."

"Unless what?"

"Well, what if we look at what happened after the event?" Molly continued with her line of thinking. "Did anyone leave town abruptly?"

"Good question. I have no idea." I ran my fingers through my auburn curls as this case rested on my chest like an elephant had decided to take a nap right on top of me. "Maybe I wasn't cut out to be a detective. This is a lot of work! Nancy Drew made it look so easy."

Evangeline, who was not a warm and fuzzy type of person, laid her hand on top of mine tenderly. "Don't get overwhelmed. I know Susan tasked you with working on this, but it's not entirely up to you. The BBPD is on the case too. You can only do what you can do. Why don't you start by exonerating all the library staff members, since Chief James seemed to think it might be an inside job? And then you can follow your lead...Camille..."

Leave it up to the cataloguer to find a logical, systematic way of doing things. I was lucky to have her on my team. "Good thinking. After lunch, I'll go talk to each one of the staff members on the attendee list. Let's see, Tom in Reference, Barbara in Circulation, and Jada in Tech Services."

"Good luck," Evangeline said after chewing her last bite of orange.

"Thanks, I have a feeling I'll need it."

※

I ambushed Tom as he was leaving his reference desk shift. Getting his interview out of the way first was a good plan because he was a talker, and I'd be able to rein him in by using the excuse of having other staff to talk to. At least that was my plan.

"Hey, Tom, do you have a moment?" I followed him from the reference desk to his office like a puppy dog.

He whipped around, his long gray ponytail following the motion and landing on his shoulder. "Sure, Sunshine. What do ya need?"

Tom was originally from Minnesota, and he had the accent to match. Friendly beyond reason, he often went on long tangents about obscure bits of history or random facts. I had a feeling he watched a lot of documentaries or something, which was perfect for a reference librarian, because you never knew what a patron was going to ask you. Reference librarians required knowledge of a little bit of everything as well as innate curiosity and a boatload of patience.

"I just want to ask you a few questions about the gala on Saturday." I held up my notepad to indicate I'd be jotting some things down.

"You betcha!" He smiled as he took a seat at his desk and gestured for me to take one of the chairs across from it.

It was very narrow, but I wiggled my generous hips into it and flipped open the notepad to the next blank page. "I know Chief James asked you some stuff yesterday..."

Tom's nose scrunched up. "Oh, no, he didn't really ask me much. We were mostly talking about our mutual interest in World War II weaponry, specifically tanks. Did you know the DD amphibious tank was crucial in our victory at Normandy?"

"Uh..." See? This was exactly how Tom sucked you into a long, meandering conversation that, while not entirely unpleasant, could certainly tick away precious minutes. I cleared my throat. "Sorry, I have others to interview, so I just want to ask you a few things."

Also, Chief James didn't really question him about the gala? I thought that was his whole point for coming into the library yesterday. He seemed to think one of us had betrayed our profession, our town—each other! Didn't that mean he swept through the building on a mission of interrogation?

"Sure, sorry. I just get really excited when it comes to history." Tom's grin grew even wider.

"Oh, that's fine, no worries." I got excited about things too. Bridgerton. Dark chocolate. Coffee. One of my YA patrons loving a book I recommended. But I had to get to the bottom of this cruel crime against the library, against my town, against my livelihood!

"Can you tell me about your night from the period of after dinner to when the Founders' Bible was stolen?" I figured I'd keep it open-ended and look for clues.

"Well, my wife and I went downstairs after dinner to mingle with the crowd and get our dance on, don'tcha know?" He chuckled as the memories appeared to dance behind his eyes. "I don't really remember anything specific until the mayor made the announcement about the donations, and then everyone was in full celebration mode—until we heard the glass shatter. I thought my heart was going to stop, my wife screamed so loud."

So that's where the scream came from. My ears were still ringing, days later.

"Did you notice anything unusual? Anyone behaving in an odd way?"

His nose wrinkled again. "Unusual or odd how? We're in a library. There's always unusual and odd stuff going on in here. Libraries are magnets for...uh...interesting people." He capped off his observation with a wink.

I couldn't argue with him there. "Did you happen to notice any of the guests wandering off to parts of the library that weren't being used for the party?" I recalibrated my question.

Tom scratched his scalp, where his gray hair was thinning, and looked up at the ceiling as he tried to access his memories from the night. "Now that you mention it, I did see those two ladies in the evening gowns...I don't know their names, I'm sorry. They seem to be friends of the mayor's wife?" he attempted to prompt me.

"Rosita and Heather," I tried to hold back my gasp. It seemed to corroborate my suspicions about Camille stealing the money and the Bible to foil her husband's chances of re-election. "Where did you see them?"

"The periodical collection on the other side of the hallway that leads to the offices," he said. "I saw some sparkles back there—turned out to be that pink dress, I think." He laughed as the picture of it filled his mind. "But I'm sure they were just having a private conversation—or, I don't know, maybe they really wanted to see the current issue of *Glamour*?"

"Or maybe they were plotting to steal our money..." My voice trailed off as I scribbled down a few notes on my pad.

Tom laughed even harder at my accusation. "I daresay, if I was going to a fundraising gala to steal a priceless artifact and the proceeds of said gala, I probably wouldn't wear such...provocative attire."

He had a point, but that could have just been part of the ruse. If accused, they could say, "Would I really wear a pink sparkling gown if I wanted to fly under the radar and steal something?"

"Thanks, Tom," I dismissed his point because I was really liking how the evidence pointed toward Camille and her Mean Girl clique. "If you think of anything else, will you let me know?"

"Of course. Good luck, Sunshine. I hope you can recover our stolen funds."

"Me too, Tom. Me too."

He lowered his chin as if to signify the seriousness of the situation. He knew as well as I did that our jobs were at stake.

Barbara, the Circulation Manager, was my next stop. She was busy training a crew of volunteers, showing them how to read the Dewey Decimal call numbers and shelve books. "Do you have a moment, or should I come back later?" I asked, leaning over the counter.

"Hey, Sunshine. Just a sec, and I'll be right with you." She instructed the volunteers to load up a cart with books and wheel it upstairs to shelve. "I'll check your work later this afternoon."

The three volunteers, elderly ladies from the community, all looked excited to be part of our mission. *See? That's what the library is all about: connecting our community with information and entertainment, and fostering a sense of belonging.* Who could possibly want to stand in the way of such noble aspirations? Only a twisted, evil, selfish person!

"What can I do for you?" Barbara straightened her shirt so the buttons aligned with the ones on her skirt. Now her buttons went in a straight line from chin to ankle, matching her personality. She was very much a by-the-book kind of person, pardon the pun, and she ran the public services area of the library with efficiency and aplomb.

"I wanted to ask you a few questions about Saturday night," I said. "Chief James probably spoke to you yesterday?"

"Why, yes, he did." Concern gripped her aging features as she clutched the pearl strand encircling her neck. "I just feel so horrible about what happened, but I'm sorry to say we weren't there at the time."

"No?" I searched her face, looking for any signs of falsehood.

"No, Stanley started feeling ill after dinner. I think he simply ate too much. He thought it was the fish at first, but when no one else seemed to be affected..."

Stanley was her husband, a short, stocky man with thick glasses and a waxy complexion. "I'm sorry to hear he didn't feel well. Is he okay now?"

She nodded, smiling in apparent gratitude. "He is fine now, thank you. Must have had to work it through his system."

That wasn't a particularly pleasant thought so soon after lunch, but I rolled with it. "What time did you leave?"

"We left around seven, not long after dinner finished up," she said. "So we missed all the hubbub. Though, in retrospect, I'm glad I wasn't there. I probably would have fainted when the Bible was stolen." She fanned herself as though she were in danger of fainting even at the thought of it. "That Bible has been our literal and symbolic connection to our town's founding for hundreds of years,

Sunshine. Donations can be replaced, but that Bible cannot."

I didn't need to be lectured about the significance of the Founders' Bible. I still remembered my first glimpse of it as a fourth-grader at Bryce Beach Elementary. We'd taken a field trip to the library to see it, and then some woman—probably a children's librarian, now that I thought about it—dressed up in colonial garb, told us the story about the founding fathers' shipwreck and how they swam to shore, then decided to settle right here in Bryce Beach. I was in awe of something that old even back then, though I couldn't begin to grasp what a treasure it truly was.

I decided not to respond to her insinuation that I didn't fully appreciate the value of what was lost. "Did you notice anyone behaving oddly before you and Stanley left?"

She shook her head. "No, it was a great evening until we had to leave." She made a *tsk-tsk* sound. "Stanley and his sensitive stomach. I've been trying to get him to see a doctor about it for many years... It's not the first time we've had to cut our evening short due to gastrointestinal distress..."

And on that note, I took my leave. I needed to track down one more library staff member who was in attendance at the gala, and that meant a trip to the bowels of the library, otherwise known as Technical Services.

Alright, so first of all, it wasn't really the bowels because it was at the back of the building. If you wanted a human body metaphor, it would be more like the feet. Or the butt, maybe? But the hallway to get there was twisty and dark, kind of like I imagined intestines being.

I pressed the buzzer button because I'd left my keys on my desk. Through the glass in the door, I saw one of the tech services staff coming to let me in. I recognized Linda O'Neal, a petite dark-haired lady who always wore denim. Lots and lots of denim.

"Hey, Sunny," she said brightly, not disappointing me in her patchwork denim skirt. They didn't get too many visitors back here unless it was someone trying to track down a missing book that was supposedly on the shelf but wasn't. And in that case, the visitor usually wasn't in the best mood.

"Sunshine," I corrected her, trying to keep the smile firmly implanted on my face. I hated being called Sunny. The only thing worse than being called Sunny was when someone made a "baking" joke about my last name. That was utterly mortifying.

"What can I do for you, Sunshine?" She emphasized my name with a tiny shred of snarkiness.

"Is Jada in?" I glanced around, seeing if I could answer the question for myself.

"No, she's still at lunch." Linda stared at me, unblinking, like she was trying to stave off an eyeroll.

Jada was one of the newer staff members at the library. Young, idealistic, and somewhat flighty, she hadn't yet developed what I would call a great rapport with her staff. My guess was they didn't think she'd paid her dues and shouldn't be a manager, but she had a brand-spankin'-new master's degree in library science, so that trumped years of experience, at least when it came to management. For better or worse.

"Any idea when she'll be back?" I added the appropriate gentle tone to this delicate question.

Linda shrugged and, yes, there was that eyeroll she'd attempted to suppress. It wormed its way out despite her best efforts. "No idea. It's Tuesday. She might not come back before her four o'clock yoga class."

I narrowed my eyes "Really? It's only one o'clock now..."

"Well, yoga is *very* important, you know..." Linda's words dripped with sarcasm.

I wondered if Susan knew about Jada's disappearing acts—it sounded like a regular thing from the picture Linda was painting. "Okay, thanks. I'll stop by tomorrow, then."

"Right. Tomorrow...well, she's leaving for vacation tomorrow," Linda disclosed.

My ears perked up as I remembered our lunch-time discussion about anyone skipping town after the event. Tomorrow would be four days after the gala, but...could this still be of significance? Jada was fresh out of library school, presumably saddled with student loan debt. Even library managers didn't make a ton of money. We certainly didn't go into this profession to get rich. Maybe she was absconding with the money and then planned to return when things died down? Of all the potential suspects in the library, Jada was the only one I didn't know well. Maybe Chief James knew what he was talking about, after all?

"Oh, okay..." I glanced down at my notepad where I'd

already crossed off my name, Molly's and Evangeline's. I drew lines through Tom's and Barbara's names. Then I drew a big fat question mark next to Jada.

I thanked Linda, Queen of Denim, for her time and headed back up to my little cubbyhole in the YA area. I supposed I should try to get some actual library work done.

But now I had two suspects...

SEVEN

Bond was sitting in the window, soaking up the last rays of late afternoon sunshine when I unlocked the door to my house. Paige slinked between my legs, welcoming me home. I breathed a deep sigh of relief now that I could finally relax, but once I brewed a cup of coffee and tried to curl up in my favorite reading nook with my new book, I found my mind wandering back to the case over and over and over again.

It didn't help that I got a text from Molly that only enabled my apparent obsession with the Bryce Beach Bandit, as I had nicknamed our perpetrator.

Molly: *Hey. Any luck this afternoon?*

Me: *Define luck.*

Molly: *Um. You want Merriam-Webster's definition or...?*

My immediate thought: *Haha for book nerd humor.*

Me: *I have a new suspect. And I want to spy on Camille, I think. Like, how do you go about doing that?*

Molly: *I think I'm the wrong person to ask.*

Me: *Pretty sure I need some spy gadgets.*

I looked over at Bond, who was staring at me from across the room, probably wondering when I was going to stop fooling around and serve him his dinner. "You got any spy gadgets, cat?"

He blinked, then continued staring.

Molly: *Here's a wild idea: you could just go talk to her?*

Me: *Like just show up at her house? The mayor's house?*

Molly: *That's what detectives always do in the movies, isn't it? They show up unannounced and catch their suspects or witnesses off-guard. That way they don't have time to prepare.*

Me: *I feel like I need a guise or something. If I don't have gadgets, I definitely need a guise.*

Molly: *What about a gal pal? Would that work?*

Me: *YES! Are you free tonight by chance?*

Molly: *No plans after dinner. Don't they live just off the boardwalk?*

Me: *They sure do.*

Molly: *Let's meet at The Candy Shoppe. I have an idea.*

Me: *You're the best!*

Molly: *See you at 7?*

Me: *I'll be there!*

B ryce Beach comprised a cove carved out between two points of coastline that jutted out into the Atlantic. On one end of the beach stood an old-fashioned lighthouse; though not in use anymore, it served as a quaint backdrop for touristy postcards and wedding photos. On the other end was a large marina and fishing pier that we shared with the next town over, which was called Berrywood.

Bryce Beach had an adorable little boardwalk, just like so many other quaint little 'burgs on the Eastern seaboard. Berrywood had one too, but ours was far superior. (Of course!) We had a half dozen nice restaurants, a few cafés, a bookstore, some clothing stores, some souvenir shops, and a few specialty shops as well, one of which was wall-to-wall candy. The Candy Shoppe was my absolute favorite place to go as a kid. *Oh, right, who am I kidding?* It was still my favorite place to go, even at forty-two. Angelo's Ristorante Italiano and The Sophisticated Bean, a fancy coffee shop, were my other favorites.

I got to the beach early because you never knew what the parking situation would be like, though a Tuesday evening in early spring was usually a safe bet. Ten years ago we never had any parking problems, but Bryce Beach was featured in one of those "best small towns in the USA" lists about a decade ago—*and we've been paying for it ever since.*

I parked my little red Mazda CX-3 on a side street, a little further from the beach. The mayor's house was only a block from my spot, so I'd be able to make a quick getaway if needed.

I didn't know what I was so worried about. I was just going to ask Camille a few questions. I'd integrate her answers with the evidence I'd collected so far—and probably overanalyze it half the night—but nothing...bad...was going to happen.

Right? I mean, this is only the most powerful couple in Bryce Beach. I'm sure I have absolutely nothing to worry about.

Despite my constant reassurances that all would be well, I decided a walk on the beach would soothe my soul before it was time to meet Molly and go on our mission. We would have invited Evangeline to join us, but she hated sand. Hated the beach. Hated being around people. So this little outing was a no-go for her.

The late April chill in the air went right into my skin, raising goosebumps all along the backs of my arms, my legs, and my neck. It was brisk, but it instilled a sense of invigoration that I desperately needed. Almost as good as a cup of coffee. *Almost.* I looked out across the water at the rolling waves, each topped with a white, lacy crown as it cascaded toward shore.

For just a split second, I imagined what it was like for Nathaniel Bryce and the other founding fathers when their ship crashed offshore. They were swimming and treading water for days before they finally caught sight of land. Can you imagine how absolutely ecstatic they were? It must have been the most wonderful sight they'd ever seen.

If I found the Founders' Bible and the missing donations from the gala, it would probably be the most wonderful sight I had ever seen. Hands down.

Glancing down at my watch, I realized it was time to meet Molly. I headed for the dune that separated the boardwalk from the beach and saw her standing there, holding what looked like a bakery box by the strings. She waved and bounced the box up and down on its elastic cord like it was bungee jumping. It looked like she'd gotten us a treat, and I was down with that. She really *was* the best.

"Hey, what's up?" I kicked the sand off my shoes as best I could but sent it flying onto her legs. "Oops, sorry."

"Thanks a lot! Here, hold this." She handed me the box and reached down to brush the sand off her legs and smooth out her skirt. She was still wearing the same clothes she'd worn to work today, just like I was. We couldn't exactly go to the mayor's house in casual attire, not when Camille had a habit of overdressing for every situation. She probably wore a dress, jewelry, full makeup and heels just to bum around the house.

"What's in the box? Something chocolate, I hope!" It felt loaded with calories, just from the weight of it.

Molly's blonde ponytail flew in the wind when she tilted her head. "It's for the mayor and his wife. To thank them for all their support of the library!" She gave me a wink.

"Ooooooohhhhh!" My friend was pretty smart. I still wished the treats were for us instead, but her plan was better.

"You know which house is theirs, right?" she asked as we started down the boardwalk toward the street where the mayor lived.

"The one with the ginormous American flag and the stone monument that spells out their last name."

"Okie dokie." We sped up our pace as the wind began to pick up, pushing us along the weathered wooden planks. The sun was setting now, and I was beginning to wish I'd listened to that "mom" voice inside my head that urged me to bring a jacket.

My heart pounded as I rang the doorbell, and then we waited. I heard dogs barking in the distance, the sound growing louder before the door handle turned. And there Camille stood, still looking as put-together as she was at the gala—not a hair out of place and her makeup perfectly applied. Just like I imagined she would be.

She made it soooo difficult to like her! Not to mention the terrible stuff Evangeline heard her say about the library.

"Sunshine?" she stammered as her eyes met mine. "Is everything okay?"

Oh... I flashed Molly a "Did you hear that?" look. Molly flashed back an "I most certainly did!" look.

"Here!" Molly lifted the box of treats. "We brought you and Mayor Steyer a gift."

"Oh, you did?" The puzzlement on her face quickly faded, and sheer delight took over. "Well, come on in! The mayor is at a town council meeting tonight—they're discussing what happened over at the library. But I can tell him you stopped by."

She opened the door and stepped back so we could enter. Two small dogs, one black, one white, flanked her as she ushered us into a sitting room. Their house was an old Victorian-style with a formal parlor anchored by an antique grandfather clock and a time-weathered grand piano decorated with a dozen or so sepia photos in ornate frames. Everything about the room was grand, in fact, from the heavy velvet drapes to the oiled bronze lamps with fabric shades trimmed in matching fringe and beads.

It wasn't exactly what I was expecting, but I didn't hate it. Especially since the back wall of the room was dominated by a marble fireplace and, on either side, massive bookcases rising nearly to the ceiling. And they were filled with books. *FILLED.* My eyes swept over the shelves in abject awe. My breath hitched when I realized I should be looking for the Founders' Bible...just in case. Then I noticed something on the floral-patterned settee and nonchalantly scooped it up.

Molly's sharp elbow poked into my side, bringing me back to reality. "Uh, we wanted to thank you for all your support of the library over the years," I told her, gesturing toward Molly, who was still holding the box of candy by its cord. "It's just a small token of our gratitude. Hope no one in the house has any allergies."

"Oh, you're so kind, ladies. Thank you so much. Of course, the library is very important to me. It holds a special place in my heart, and I was just devastated to see what happened there on Saturday night." She laid it on thick, her lips pooched out in a sad pout as she took the box from Molly and set it on the table.

"Yeah, I just don't know what we're going to do without that money," Molly said. "I think they might need to let one of our staff members go. Either that, or we won't be able to add to our collections this year."

"Our boss says that if our budgets continue to be slashed, our doors will be closed within five years," I added. She hadn't said that, but you know, embellishing the truth is okay when you're trying to solve a crime. *Right, Lord?*

"That's a horribly sad thought." Camille sighed as though it was a possibility completely outside of her control. "Well, I certainly do appreciate you ladies stopping by. I'm sure Bull will be thrilled to have some treats in the house since I don't buy that sort of thing." She trailed her fingers down her trim figure, the earlier traces of sympathy vanishing into thin air.

"Hey, I have a question for you," I stopped her midstride as she was beginning to make her way toward the door to usher us out.

Her eyebrow rose as she glared at me, but she didn't say a word.

"Where did you go during your husband's speech?" I asked. "You know, when we were in the workroom counting the money, you said he needed you by his side to make the announcement, but then you slipped down the hallway when I handed him the Post-It note with the final tally on it."

Her cheeks flushed ever so slightly, and her body stiffened. My gaze darted over to Molly to see if she caught the reaction. Her narrowed eyes proved she had.

"I had the fish for dinner," she said after sucking in a deep breath. "It didn't agree with me..."

"So you were in the restroom?" Molly questioned.

Camille let out a humorless chuckle. "Not that it's any of your business, but, yes."

Though Barbara's husband Stanley also had some...
uh...challenges after eating the fish, I didn't buy Camille's
story for a second. But how could I prove she'd taken the
money? And the Bible? I was sure her little clique stole
the Bible to create a distraction while she absconded with
the money. I strained every cell in my memory, trying to
recall how long she was gone. She had reappeared at her
husband's side by the time the police arrived. So she had
stashed the Bible and money somewhere? But where?

"I'm just curious...do you have any idea who might
have done it?" I switched tactics. "Stolen the Bible and
money, I mean?"

She scoffed, her caramel-blonde waves rustling
around her shoulders. She gathered her hair in her fist,
raked her fingers through it, and smoothed it to one side.
A couple of strands floated to the floor. "It's not my job to
speculate about suspects. That's the police's job."

"But surely you have a theory," I pressed. "Everyone
does, you know." Would peer pressure work on someone
like the mayor's wife?

Camille straightened her spine and looked from me
to Molly and back again, then she leaned forward as
though she was going to let us in on a big secret. "Actually, I do have some concerns..."

"Concerns?" I stared at her. It seemed like a strange,
benign word to use for the tragedy that occurred
Saturday night at the gala.

"Yes," she continued, "about Willa." She pursed her
lips and nodded as though the whole situation had kept
her up at night.

"Willa Bryce Monroe?" Molly clarified.

"Yes." She let out a long, dramatic sigh. "I overheard Bull talking on the phone with her the other day, and it appears she's not doing as well financially as she would have everyone believe. Something about stocks...or...I don't know..." She waved her hand through the air as though apologizing for her vagueness. "I know it sounds crazy, but I think she passed off a bad check—she gave a pretty sizeable donation, did she not?"

I nodded, remembering the look of her signature scrawled across the line. It was shaky, like that of a frail, elderly woman. She had to be nearing her eightieth birthday, if she wasn't older. How in the world would she have pulled off the greatest heist in Bryce Beach history?

"So, let me get this straight," I said as my hands involuntarily flew to my hips, "you think the richest woman in town—a descendent of the folks who signed the Bible that's been revered by our community for hundreds of years—stole the gala donations and the town's most valuable piece of history to cover up the fact she wrote a bad check?"

Camille shrugged. "Stranger things have happened. Why? What do you think happened?" she snapped.

Molly grabbed my arm, undoing my indignant propped-hip pose that was starting to feel rather powerful and self-righteous, and tugged me toward her. "We should get going," she hissed in my ear.

"Sorry, we have to go," I stated as though Camille hadn't heard my friend's stage whisper. "Hope you enjoy the treats. Thanks again for your support!"

I threw a glance over my shoulder at the mayor's wife as Molly rushed me through the foyer and down the porch steps to the sidewalk. "What?!" I shrieked as soon as we were a couple houses past the mayor's.

"I was afraid you were going to accuse her of stealing the funds!" Molly admitted. "It was on the tip of your tongue; I could just feel it."

I scoffed, "Whatever. I'm way smoother than that. I'm super smooth."

"Is that so?" Molly stopped and pinned her gaze on me. The streetlights had come on, and we were standing right in their spotlight. We were definitely not nailing the "keep a low profile" thing.

"Yes...because I got this." I held up a strand of hair that I'd plucked off the settee.

"What is that?" Molly scrubbed her hand down her face like it had been the longest day of her life. Next to Saturday, this day was probably a close second. "An invisible clue?"

"You might not be able to tell in this light, but it's a strand of Camille's hair." I wanted to add "so there," but I refrained. *Because I'm smooth.*

"What's that going to prove?" she asked as we started to walk again.

"Well...you know as well as I do that Camille didn't count any of the money."

"True..."

"So how would she know about Mrs. Monroe's donation?"

"Ohhhh..."

"And have you noticed she has a habit of touching her hair? Running her fingers through it?"

I could tell the moment it dawned on my friend

where I was going with this line of questioning. Her mouth opened in a perfectly round O shape as a little gasp slipped out. "So if there's a hair in the workroom..."

"Exactly. I'll check tomorrow first thing in the morning. I just hope they haven't vacuumed in there yet."

Molly looked thoughtful for a second. "Frieda vacuums the office area on Thursdays, so you should be okay if you get in there tomorrow. Do you think the police found any fingerprints or hair at the scene?"

"I don't know, but if I find a hair, and it matches this sample...I might need to go have a little chat with Chief James..."

EIGHT

My worry about not being able to sleep due to thinking of the case became a self-fulfilling prophecy. Wednesday morning, after my second cup of coffee, I finally gathered the strength to pull myself out of bed, but not before scouring my notepad and taking a fresh look at my list of suspects.

I had been able to eliminate some of the townsfolk after looking them up on social media to verify who they were and their roles in the community. It wasn't a very scientific process of elimination, but Ruth Painter, the Sunday school teacher, and Dr. Schulz, the pediatrician, didn't seem like very likely suspects. There were a few others I nixed as well. I could always revisit them if my leads didn't pan out.

I was still stuck on Camille—and possibly Jada, I needed to find out more about this alleged vacation she was on—but then what Camille said about Willa Bryce Monroe was buzzing around my head like a pesky bee after your soda at a picnic. The only thing I couldn't get past was *how*.

The perpetrator of the crime needed motive, opportunity, and means. The *motive* might have been there for Mrs. Monroe, if she truly was having financial difficulties and didn't want anyone to know, and she obviously had the *opportunity* to commit the crime at the gala, same as everyone else who was there. But what about the *means*? She was a little old lady who walked with a cane. I couldn't imagine her breaking a glass display case. And how would she have stolen the money? I supposed she could have hired someone, or maybe she had an accomplice?

After my third cup of coffee, I remembered that every morning, Willa Bryce Monroe took her Pomeranian for a little jaunt down her street. She went about two blocks, passing in front of the library, and then she made the return trip home. She was slow, anchoring herself with her cane, and her pup liked to sniff out every morsel of even remote interest along the way, so it was often a twenty- to thirty-minute endeavor. I passed her on my way into work all the time.

If I hurried, I could catch her this morning.

My energy was renewed by the prospect of interviewing the wealthy widow—or maybe it was just the caffeine finally hitting my system. I brushed my teeth, showered, and put on a lemon-yellow dress with little pink flowers. It just screamed spring to me, and with sunny, blue skies greeting us on this May the first, it seemed like the perfect outfit.

Instead of parking in the library lot, I whipped into a

space at the coffee shop on the corner about two blocks from the boardwalk. It wasn't The Sophisticated Bean, which was actually on the boardwalk, but this one was my second favorite in town. Bryce Beach definitely had its fair share of coffee shops per capita, and I was more than okay with that. I had time to top off my tank with one more caffeine infusion before I was due at work, and besides, one glance down the block told me Mrs. Monroe hadn't begun her morning constitutional just yet.

After ordering a café mocha from my favorite barista, Jennie, I headed for the door, composing a little prayer in my head. *Give me the right words to say to Mrs. Monroe, Lord. I just want to get to the bottom of this so the library can move on, so our whole town can move forward. And I want to get Your Word back too, of course...so any help you can throw my way would be most appreciated...*

I closed it out with my normal *in Jesus' name, amen*— all in my head, of course—and the tinkle of the bells on the coffee shop door almost sounded like He was giving me an answer. I hoped it was the answer I wanted as I spotted the small, hunched-over figure; a roving, sniffing puppy on a leash; and a cane.

Leaving my car in the lot—I could come back for it at lunchtime—I strolled down the sidewalk trying to behave as normally and casually as possible. *I'm just on my way to work,* I reminded myself. *Nothing suspicious or note-worthy about that!*

"Good morning, Mrs. Monroe," I said from a few feet away as I approached her. Her little brown and white dog instantly reared up on his hind legs, trying to reach me.

"You can pet him," she assured me. "He's friendly."

I bent down and offered my hand to the pup, who went wild sniffing Bond and Paige all over my skin. I patted his head. "Good boy! What's his name?"

"Natty." Willa Bryce Monroe's pale gray eyes crinkled with deep lines as she smiled. "He's named after my great-great-great-great-great...well, you know, lots of greats...grandfather, Nathaniel Bryce."

She acted like I wasn't aware she was the only known living descendent of our town's founder. *Only someone who isn't from Bryce Beach or has been living under a rock their entire life wouldn't know that!*

"That's a great name!" I stroked the dog's fur, and he licked me in appreciation. "A great name for a great dog!"

She was beaming now, basking in the praise I'd given her little creature. Then she stopped abruptly, a scowl taking the place of the grin she'd worn. "Have you found my ancestors' Bible yet? You work at the library, don't you? You were there on Saturday night—at the party—weren't you?"

She threw so many questions at me, I wasn't sure which to answer first. And it was ironic considering I was the one who meant to ask *her* questions. Maybe she was getting her Nancy Drew on too?

"I do work at the library, ma'am, and no, we haven't found the Bible yet. The police are investigating it."

"Police-schmolice," she scoffed. "Chief James couldn't find a hole on the ground if it was his own grave, and he was standing in it!"

Wow, now that was a colorful remark. But, finally, someone who wasn't gaga over the chief? Maybe I had more in common with this Willa Bryce Monroe character than I'd thought. And she was indeed a character!

"I'm working on it too, actually," I let her in on the secret. Maybe she would volunteer some information?

"Well, that is nice to hear, my girl." She reached out and took my hand into her old, weathered, wrinkly one. "Such a nice girl, dearie. And look at that bright red hair! Now, is there a Mr. Sunshine?"

A nervous laugh bubbled up my throat. I didn't know if it was weirder that she wanted to know if I was single or that she remembered my name. "I'm not married, no, ma'am."

"Oh, that's a shame, my dear. Marriage is the most wonderful institution God ever created—next to the church, you know. Of course, you're a little pudgy to find a husband now. You might want to work on that." She patted my hand as though her simple suggestion was likely to change my life.

I wasn't a stranger to strangers offering unsolicited dieting and weight loss advice. I'd been a fat girl my whole life, and for some reason people thought my weight was a public matter. Ten years ago, I would have run home crying if someone said that to me, but I was older and wiser in my forties. Plus, I was beginning to think this woman was a little off her rocker, maybe. If that was the case, she probably wasn't the mastermind behind the Bryce Beach Bandit. Which only pointed the finger of blame more solidly in Camille Steyer's direction!

"Back in my day, you got married when you were under twenty, mind you. If you didn't have a beau by twenty-one?" she rambled on. "Well, then, you were probably destined for spinsterhood. I was one of the lucky ones, of course, but then again, I was beautiful back in the day. And I had a lovely figure. Always turned the fellas' heads. Didn't hurt that my daddy had a lot of money. He was the mayor back then, you know.

"I probably could have been the mayor if I'd wanted to, dearie. But my husband wouldn't hear of it! He's passed on now, of course. But Mr. Monroe had very traditional ideas about what women should do with their lives, and it involved cooking, baking, cleaning, and child birthing. I did plenty of those things in my day, my dear. Of course, we always had a housekeeper and a cook. And my two little ones had a nanny. But—"

She went on and on and on. I didn't think she had any heirs, but I didn't want to pry. Besides, I was going to be late for work if she kept on yapping. However, I tried to listen carefully because she knew a lot about the town, and maybe she'd reveal something valuable, something that might provide some insight on the case.

"That mayor of ours, what's his name, Bull or something equally ridiculous? I don't trust him or that tart of a wife any farther than I could throw them. They aren't good Christians, you know!"

"They're not?" I gasped, surprised that the conversation had turned to them when Camille was still my primary suspect. I was definitely all ears now. "They go to church every Sunday."

"Well, have you seen the hems on that woman's skirts? She gives the whole town a free peep at her goods, my dear. It's obscene, I tell you. And that man. Well, everyone knows he's running around on her with

Francesca down at the Bryce Beach Boutique. He's a notorious philanderer. You know he got his high school girlfriend in trouble and had to marry her, and then he cheated on her with the new wife. My son Nathaniel was in his class. He can tell you all about it—"

"Did you see Mayor Steyer and his wife at the gala on Saturday?" I knew for a fact she did because I saw them talking. She, of course, had looked perfectly agreeable and happy to speak with them then.

"I did, my dear. And that dress the wife was wearing...it was a little much, wasn't it?" She shook her head. I had to laugh at how she always called Camille "the wife" instead of her name. "Now you, on the other hand. You wore red, did you not?"

She definitely had a better memory than I'd given her credit for. Maybe she wasn't off her rocker?

"I did wear red," I confirmed, equal parts afraid and excited to hear her fashion critique.

"That dress was flattering to your figure. You should wear that type of waistline more often. It de-emphasizes the hips."

Welp, we were back to discussing my body. How fun! Not.

"Well, you looked mighty lovely," she continued, "even if redheads aren't supposed to wear red. That's an outdated notion, anyway, dearie." She nodded as though she was a world-renowned fashion expert. This coming from a woman who was still wearing dresses from the Carter administration.

"Did you see anything unusual at the party on Saturday?" I changed the subject. Maybe she had seen Camille sneak off to the offices right before the Bible was stolen and the money disappeared. It would be quite amusing if Camille implicated her, and she implicated Camille.

"That dark-haired, vampire-looking woman you were with, the one in the purple dress. You were with her and a blonde," Mrs. Monroe said, her voice taking on a bit more of a *tremolo* quality than her normal elderly lady voice.

"Evangeline Dupree?" I narrowed my gaze as I stared her down, waiting for her to elaborate. "What about her?"

"She is pure evil, that woman," the widow hissed. Then she looked all around herself, as though a spirit might appear out of thin air and snatch her up in its icy grip.

"Pure evil?" I couldn't help but chuckle. "Evangeline is a grumpy cataloguer, but she's not pure evil."

"You should stay away from her, dearie. You are the light, and she is the dark. The deep, dark abyss. The evil abyss." Now she was scaring me with her wide, round eyes and wavering voice.

I was quickly reverting to my earlier off-the-rocker theory now.

"She stole the Bible," Mrs. Monroe insisted. "Mark my words. She is using it in her witchcraft!"

"What?" First of all, I was pretty sure Evangeline was standing right next to Molly when the glass display case shattered. And she was just as shocked as everyone else.

Natty the Dog was straining against his leash, ready to move on with the rest of his morning walk. I'd already watched him pee on the library's property, and I was afraid at this point if I didn't let Mrs. Monroe get back to it, he'd leave us a nice, stinky present right beside our entrance. What a way to welcome patrons to the library, huh?

"That's an interesting theory, Mrs. Monroe," I said. "I better let you get back to your walk now. It was nice talking to you."

"You too, dearie!" Her face brightened as though she hadn't just called one of my best friends a witch. "If you want any diet recipes, let me know! I have a great cookbook you can borrow."

Alrighty then. "Um, thanks. Have a good day!"

I briskly passed by her, my footsteps pounding into the sidewalk before I reached the library steps. Then I raced up them and into the building, wondering if I would burst before I could go share with Evangeline what Willa Bryce Monroe said about her.

I headed directly back to the technical services office area, letting myself in with my key this time. After marching straight to Evangeline's cataloguing lair, I found her door closed and the office light off. My eyes darted around the open area with its cubicles in the center.

Linda O'Neal, wearing a plaid skirt with a denim jacket (of course), came out, shaking her head. "Who're you looking for this time, Sunny?

I cringed at her use of my solely-father-approved nickname. "Sunshine," I corrected her. "Have you seen Evangeline today?"

"Nope, sorry. With her and Jada gone, it's quiet back here. Then again, when the cat's away, the mice will play!"

I wasn't sure what tech services workers considered "playing." Maybe ripping the little perfume samples out of the magazines before shelving them? Having book cart races? It didn't look like anything at all was going on back there. *Ah, maybe that's the point.*

I weaved my way back into the main part of the library, toward the circulation desk. I glanced past the counter to the office area where Tom and the other reference librarian, Jessica, had private offices for when they weren't at the reference desk.

Barbara entered the area from the circulation desk, carrying a hefty stack of books. She set them down on a cart and sighed. "You'd think with as many books as I lift a day, I'd be stronger."

I smiled at her self-deprecating humor, but then I remembered why I'd rushed back there. Of all the library staff members, Barbara was the most likely to know where someone was or be up on the latest happenings. "Have you seen Evangeline today? She's not in her office."

"No, actually, I think she called in sick." Barbara turned and called out to the circulation desk worker. *So much for being quiet in the library!* "Hey, did you answer the phone when the cataloguer called in?"

I heard a mumbled response but didn't catch what she said.

"Yeah, she's sick today," Barbara repeated.

Weird. She didn't even tell me. I'd have to text her later to check in on her. "Alright, thanks for letting me know."

"Sure thing. How's the sleuthing going?" Her lips

tilted up into a crooked smile, and it was painfully obvious she was patronizing me.

"It's going great! Thanks for asking." I forced a smile, and that was enough to send her scurrying off to whatever task she was trying to accomplish.

Evangeline is sick? She seemed fine yesterday. I'd have to ask Molly if she'd heard from her.

The hair! I suddenly remembered as I was walking toward the offices on the back wall. Between Tom's office and Jessica's was the workroom where we'd counted the money at the gala. I patted my purse, where I'd put the hair in a baggie so I could easily compare it to any specimen I collected here. I glanced around to make sure I wasn't being watched. One of the advantages of having an understaffed library was that there wasn't anyone around to catch me snooping in the workroom.

Scoping out that room from top to bottom, I gave it the old Sherlock Holmes treatment—the only thing missing was an old-fashioned magnifying glass. And, to my great disappointment, I didn't find a single hair or any other clue that would help me solve the case.

Scrubbing my hands in the restroom across the hall from the back entrance to the offices, I tried to buoy my sinking heart. I wasn't sure why I was so invested in the idea of finding the smoking gun—er, hair—but I was. I feared Susan was probably correct about the police. Once the case went cold, they would stop looking. And if Camille Steyer was our thief, they'd never even think to bark up that tree.

"Alright," I told myself—out loud, because I talked to myself on occasion, "I should just go get some work done." I had a backlog of new YA books to shelve, and I wanted to create a summer reading display. It was only May first, but these things took time, and I wanted it to be perfect. I also wanted to come up with some sort of summer reading incentive that would bring my YA peeps inside the building. If my job was on the line, I wanted to prove to Susan that I could bring patrons in and that we had a substantial YA footprint. In other words, I was looking for a miracle.

I noticed Anna Cooper browsing the new additions shelf—the one I needed to update.

"Hey, Anna!" I greeted her, entering the YA space like the cheery ray of Sunshine my parents intended me to be when they gave me such a ridiculous name. "Shouldn't you be in school?"

"We're off today," she answered, not even glancing away from the books. It was like her eyes were glued to them, and she couldn't tear them away. *Sigh.* She and I understood each other. Two peas in a pod. "The teachers had some sort of professional development day."

"Gotcha." I glanced around the space, wishing more teens came to the library on their day off from school. *This place should be packed on a day like this!* Maybe if we recovered the gala donations, I could order some video game consoles? That would surely be a hit.

I turned back to Anna. "I'm pretty sure you've read all the books on that shelf, but I have some new ones I was getting ready to put out."

She turned to me with huge, sparkling eyes, her mouth practically salivating at the prospect of shiny, glossy new books. It was like she was an addict, and I was offering her a fix. *Not that I know anything at all about drugs, but that's how it works, right?*

"Really?" Her whole face was lit up.

I was pretty sure I'd made this kid's day. Maybe her whole week.

"Yes, ma'am! Come here, and I'll show you what I've got." I beckoned her with my index finger, and she followed me over to my desk like she was in a trance. I unlocked my storage closet and wheeled out the cart of new books I'd been hoarding back there, waiting for the start of the month.

She licked her lips, collecting the drool, as she started to peruse the spines of the books, all lined up in a neat row with their dust jackets shiny and new. She pulled one off and scanned the blurb on the back, her lips spreading into an excited grin. By the time she was done, she had chosen four of my eight new books.

Only eight, I lamented. We really needed that money so I could get some new books for summer. And video game consoles, apparently.

"These are awesome!" she squealed as she set them down on my desk. Then her enthusiasm withered away like leaves on a tree in November. "I heard what happened on Saturday night." She turned her head toward the lobby, where the empty space that had once held the Founders' Bible looked so barren and ugly. A spotlight shone down on the empty tile floor from the chandelier above, further highlighting the depressing sight.

"Yeah, we're pretty bummed." I downplayed it...a lot. No need to get this teen all depressed, right?

"Is it true they stole all the money that was donated?"

I nodded. "Yeah, but the police are working on recovering it." I scanned each of her books and printed out the due date slip, sliding it under the cover of the book on top.

She sighed. "I put ten bucks in that donation box."

That was like a stab through my heart. She was only thirteen, so I was sure ten dollars was a significant amount of money for her, showing how she revered the library and wanted to support my efforts. "I'm so sorry, Anna. Here, do you want me to pay you back?" I reached for my purse in the closet I'd unlocked earlier.

"Oh, no, of course not. I just was hoping it would go to buy more books." Her face brightened a little. "Hope the police come through for us."

I liked how she used the word "us." Our entire community had been robbed. I wished I had more faith in the police, but Chief James seemed so dispassionate when he was in here on Monday. And he seemed convinced that one of us had betrayed the library.

I looked around the first floor as Anna scooped up her books and stuffed them in her bag. Barbara and one of her staff members smiled at me from the circulation desk. Tom, across the floor in the adult area, was busy helping a patron at the reference desk. Molly was doing a story time for preschoolers by the big windows overlooking the courtyard.

My colleagues were good, honest, hard-working people. They loved the library. They weren't traitors!

"Hey," Anna said, pulling my attention away from my thoughts. She rearranged her long braids over her shoulder, smoothing them down against her tawny skin like she was a little nervous to say whatever was on her mind. "I just remembered... I promised to tell you that my older sister Liz is looking for a summer job. She's a wiz with computer stuff, like she even won some big hacking contest. It was in the paper and everything. So if you need any help with your website or anything tech-related around here...she'd be thrilled to work here. And she'd probably be a lot cheaper than other tech people since she's only sixteen."

I smiled at Anna, who was so kind to look out for the library's tech needs and her sister's need for a job. Though maybe she just wanted her big sis out of her hair for the summer; it was hard to say.

"That's good to know, thanks. If we have the funds for something like that, I'd definitely consider hiring her. Can you have her send her resume to me?" I handed her one of my business cards with my email address.

She tucked it into one of the new books she'd checked out. "Thanks, Ms. Baker. I'll let her know."

"Enjoy the books, Anna!"

Her bright grin from earlier returned full-force. "I will!"

NINE

Thursday, and I was no closer to solving this mystery. I'd thought about trying to tail Camille Steyer, see if I could figure out what she'd done with the money and/or Founders' Bible, but I had an appointment in the afternoon, and I was pretty sure it would be hard for someone with my stature and hair color to sneak around stealthily. If I was going to make a habit of sleuthing, I probably needed to invest in some disguises.

"Hey you!" I called across the quiet library, crossing toward the children's section.

"Hey you!" Molly called back, her head tilted and a bewildered look on her face. "I was looking for you yesterday before close, but you'd already left for the day."

The dad in the corner trying to pick out a book with his son shot me a dirty look. *Yeah, yeah. Librarians are supposed to be doing the shushing, not the patrons.* I was well aware. It was remarkable how many times I'd been shushed during my library career.

"I had a doctor's appointment yesterday and needed to leave early," I explained, lowering my voice. "But I texted last night and didn't hear back from you."

"I went to bed early, and just got in this morning, so I figured I might as well talk to you in person."

"Gotcha. Well, we need to chat."

"Yes we do," she agreed. "You first."

"Evangeline," I breathed out.

"Yeah! What's her deal? She never replied to my text!" Molly's petite features scrunched up with dismay.

"Mine either. Barbara said she called in sick yesterday, which isn't like her at all." Just putting that together made chills dance up my spine. I hadn't ever known her to be sick, in fact, and I'd been working with her for ten years. I'd known her even longer than I'd known Molly.

"According to Tom," Molly said, her face pinched with concern, a mirror of mine, "the only time Evangeline has missed work that wasn't for a vacation day was the day her divorce was finalized, and she had to go to the courthouse to sign the papers."

"Wow. That must have been before I knew her." Evangeline had been divorced from someone she called "DW" for as long as I could remember. I wasn't sure what DW stood for, but I had a feeling it wasn't his actual name.

"Well..." Molly tapped her fingertips on the surface of her desk as she stabbed me with her gaze, waiting to see how I would interpret our friend's mysterious absence.

"She was standing right with us when it happened,

wasn't she?" I knew where she was going with that look, and I didn't like it. Not one bit.

"You were standing with the mayor," Molly reminded me.

"Oh, right." I closed my eyes and brought up a visual of Saturday night. I had an almost-photographic memory. I often closed my eyes and replayed things I'd seen—if I could access the data in my cluttered mind. It was like an episode of *Hoarders* in there.

There I was, standing by Mayor Steyer as he read the figure off the pink Post-It note I'd given him. I could see the figure clearly written in my own handwriting in blue ink. The mayor smelled like aftershave and garlic—not a great combination, but I was grinning and bearing it. I was pretty stoked about the figure on that Post-It note, and I was watching the faces of the crowd react as he read it off. There was shock followed by elation, and I was surprised at how even the older and more stoic members of our community got so excited.

I tried to pick out Evangeline in the crowd, but I didn't see her. I saw Molly. But no Evangeline.

"Was she with you?" I stared at Molly, hoping her answer would be yes.

"She said she left her coat upstairs in the activities room," Molly answered, making my heart sink. "I didn't think anything of it at the time. I watched her go up the stairs..."

"But she could have come back down the lobby staircase..." My hand flew to my face, where I spread my fingers out over my forehead, trying to ward off the migraine that was starting to brew behind my skull.

"She already knew the figure on the Post-It note. So there was no reason for her to stick around for the announcement," Molly conjectured.

"Right. And she isn't big on celebrations...or happiness in general."

"Or people."

"The fact she was even *at* the gala is pretty much a miracle." As soon as I said it, my eyes bugged out, and my mouth popped open.

"Oh no," Molly gasped.

I shook my head rapidly, refusing to believe it. "But she had to have an accomplice, right? How could she get from the lobby to the workroom and then back to the party so fast?"

"Well, she could have bolted for the circulation desk right after she smashed the case and took the Bible. Maybe she hid behind the counter until the crowd moved into the lobby to check out the commotion; then she could have entered the offices from behind the counter. Maybe she went into the workroom, nabbed the money, exited out the back and stashed it somewhere. Then she rejoined the party and went back for the money later," Molly theorized. "She has keys to the building. She could have even come back the next day for it. We don't open till noon on Sundays."

I hated to admit it, but it was definitely plausible. The fact that we didn't have security cameras was coming back to bite us in the rear end yet again! I scrambled for something, anything, that would exonerate my friend. "So here's a question..."

"What's that?" Molly's eyebrow rose.

"When she said she needed to go upstairs to get her coat...did she actually return with a coat?"

Molly scratched her head for a moment before the color drained from her already pale face. "She was wearing a big heavy sweater over her purple dress. She didn't bring a coat."

Before I could bring up the fact that Jada from Tech Services was also gone, and that there was a chance they were in cahoots—they were friends—I heard the phone on my desk ringing across the room. Molly shot me a worried look as I rushed over to answer it.

"Hello?" I could see it was my boss's extension as I dove for the receiver.

"Oh, there you are," she said. "I've been trying to reach you."

"You have? I've been here all morning," I stated, not meaning to sound defensive but definitely sounding defensive.

"Can you come up to my office please?"

"Sure, of course." My heartbeat picked up its pace as I made my way back over to Molly, who was frozen there with her hands in a *Well?* position.

"Susan," I said when I reached her. It looked like the father and son were about ready to check out, so I couldn't elaborate. "Should I tell her?"

"No," Molly insisted, shaking her head adamantly. "Let's go talk to Evangeline after work."

"Okay." I shot her a thumbs-up, then headed to see Susan, feeling very much like I'd been called to the principal's office in high school, though I never actually had because I was a model, straight-A student. But I was pretty sure this was what it would feel like.

"Jesus, take the wheel," I muttered under my breath as I pushed her door open.

"Hey, Sunshine. Have a seat." Her tone was neutral, but my heart was still pounding like I'd run a sprint instead of just climbing the stairs.

"What can I do for you?" I folded my hands in my lap and tried to project a very businesslike attitude. My eyes ran over the bookcases behind her desk. On the third shelf from the top, a book called *Anagrams, Crosswords, and Word Games* was pulled out about two inches farther than the rest. I had to resist my strong librarian urge to push it back in to make it even with the rest of the spines.

"How is your investigation going?" Susan asked as she pushed away from her desk and crossed one leg over the other. She smoothed down her black trousers with one hand even though there weren't any wrinkles in them.

"Uh...well..." I decided to go with my lead about Camille because I still couldn't believe Evangeline would be involved in something so sinister. I couldn't imagine her motivation—unless she was actually a witch like Willa Bryce Monroe suggested yesterday when I saw her and Natty the Dog on their morning walk.

"Everything okay?" Susan brought her hand to the desktop and started to tap her fingers impatiently.

"I went to see the mayor's wife the other night..." I took out my notepad where I'd been tracking all the suspects, my hunches, and any evidence I'd collected. It wasn't much so far, but at least I killed some time opening the cover and appearing to pore over my notes before I had to address her.

"Camille Steyer?" My boss's eyebrow arched as she pinned her dark beady gaze on me.

"Yes." I sucked in a deep breath, preparing to spill my secret suspect. "Evangeline overheard Mrs. Steyer telling her friends that she hated the library, and she really hoped her husband wouldn't be re-elected this year."

I wasn't expecting Susan's reaction. She threw back her head with laughter. "Oh, yes, it's quite well known that Camille hates the library and doesn't want Bull to win another term, but she's been saying that for years. Then he keeps on winning. He's on, what, his third term now? They really need to set term limits..."

"What? Why would she say that and be on the Friends of the Library committee? Actually *chair* the committee!" I scoffed.

"Ever hear the phrase 'keep your friends close and your enemies closer'?" Susan was still chuckling loud enough she almost appeared to wipe a tear out of the corner of her eye, but I knew that must not be the case. She rarely ever smiled, let alone laughed. And she most certainly didn't cry. That conversation we'd had about the case on Monday was the most upset I'd ever seen her, and she still wasn't worked up enough to cry.

I still preferred the idea of Camille in the role of Bryce Beach Bandit over my good friend Evangeline. I refused to let go of it that easily. "She openly tells people she hates the library and doesn't want to be the mayor's wife?"

"That's right," Susan confirmed. "Bull keeps getting

re-elected because he does a decent job and usually runs unopposed. Or his competition is some fruitcake out-of-towner no one trusts."

In our town, "out-of-towner" could refer to anyone who wasn't physically born at the Bryce Beach Hospital. If your parents moved here when you were the ripe old age of one day, you came from an out-of-towner family.

I still had my suspicions about Camille, no matter what Susan said. But I was willing to entertain any other suspects who weren't Evangeline. "When I went to talk to the mayor's wife the other night, she expressed that Willa Bryce Monroe might be a person of interest."

No uproarious chuckle this time, but instead a loud snort. "Willa? Oh, come on, now, Sunshine. You've been here long enough to know that Willa is our biggest donor. And I heard she really outdid herself this year."

"That's just it. Camille said she overheard her husband speaking with Willa, and she revealed that she'd fallen on hard times as of late. Maybe she stole the money so she wouldn't have to deal with the embarrassment of not donating or passing a bad check. You know, 'cause she wanted to keep up appearances."

It sounded pretty silly when I said it out loud, but after talking with the woman, I honestly couldn't rule it out. She might not have been completely incapacitated, but she was definitely working with some miswired circuits.

"Well, the checks have been cashed," Susan revealed. "At least one of them has, anyway. And it was hers. So that blows your theory."

"What do you mean it was cashed?" My mouth

dropped open as I stared at her. "How is that possible? Not into the library account, right?" For a split second, hope burst like fireworks on my face.

"It was uploaded via some banking app to a bank in the Cayman Islands." Her face was completely neutral, hands folded in front of her on her desk.

Cayman Islands? Who the Helvetica would do that? "How do you know?"

"Chief James called me this morning. Willa's check was deposited into an account in the Cayman Islands, but they haven't been able to match it to any suspects yet. They're looking into it. They have to deal with the Cayman Islands police, and apparently that's a challenge."

"Just that one check was deposited?" It seemed suspicious to me that it was just one' check when we'd collected dozens, but maybe that would be the only one cashed. The others were much smaller. So maybe the thief figured if they could pocket the cash, which wasn't an insignificant amount since we'd had a donation box sitting out for the entire month of April, and that one check, the heist had a good pay-off.

Susan shrugged her broad shoulders. "So far that's all I know. They're still working on it."

"Were they going to tell me?" My face flushed with anger as I struggled to suck in enough air to fill my lungs. "I thought I was supposed to be in the loop?" Why didn't Chief James call me? Maybe he disliked me as much as I disliked him.

She shrugged. "He called me instead, I guess. Even

though I told him you were the point person since you were in charge of the gala."

If I didn't already have a beef with Chief James, I was burning with rage at him at the moment. *Lord*, I prayed, *please help me calm down*. My "Jesus, take the wheel" plea from earlier didn't seem to be working. Almost like He took the wheel and went in the complete opposite direction of where I wanted to go.

If Willa's check was deposited, it didn't exonerate her exactly. What if she deposited her own check from one account to another in the Cayman Islands? Wasn't a rich person more likely to have a bank account in a foreign country, anyway?

"So, besides Camille Steyer," Susan said, "who else is on your radar?"

I swallowed enough air to give me stomach pains later. "Well, uh, the other suspect I have is someone in the library, unfortunately."

Susan's lips set into a long, thin line as she looked at me, her gray-green eyes taking on an icy glare.

"Hear me out, okay?" I knew it was a longshot, but...

I was just starting to work up the moxie to tell her about how Jada suspiciously went on vacation right after the gala, but then I remembered I'd seen something in the workroom a couple years ago when Evangeline and I were trying to clean it out—things were slow over holiday break, if I recalled correctly, and we volunteered to organize stuff in there. Maybe we were brown-nosing. Maybe we just needed a break from our normal daily grind, but...

"Well, spit it out, Sunshine," Susan admonished me.

"I remember seeing a stamp in the workroom once

upon a time. A long time ago. Just one of those rubber stamps, but it was for endorsing checks. It said 'For Deposit Only. Bryce Beach Library.' And there was a place to sign underneath."

My boss pursed her lips as she stared at me, presumably waiting for me to finish.

When she didn't say anything or offer any kind of comment, I rushed out, "Let me run downstairs and see if I can find it."

"I'll be here." She crossed her arms over her chest as though she relished the idea of me going on a wild goose chase while she waited.

I ran down the stairs as fast as my chubby legs would carry me, across the space between the reference area and circulation desk, where the DJ had been set up on Saturday night, then down the hallway to the right of the circulation desk, where the restrooms and the entrance to the offices were.

We kept the door locked all the time, so I whipped out my keys and opened it. We didn't have newfangled tech like ID cards that opened the doors, though maybe after this security failure we'd get them? *Nah, too expensive.* We probably wouldn't get cameras either, knowing how frugal Susan was.

No one was around, which I found comforting as I dashed into the workroom and began to throw open the drawers built into the counter that was anchored to the wall. Above it were shelves with supplies like different colors and weights of paper and envelopes. As I was madly tearing through every single drawer, I heard footsteps behind me and the door close.

The blood in my veins froze as I slowly swiveled around to see who had followed me inside and shut the door. The click resounded through my ears like a gun had been cocked. I didn't know why I was so panicky, but I couldn't take the chance that the thief wouldn't revisit the crime scene to try to prevent me from discovering his or her identity.

But all that adrenaline was for naught.

Standing right there in her lavender dress and sensible pumps was Molly, shaking her blonde head at me in apparent amusement. "What'cha doing?"

"Uh, looking for something?" *Stupid questions deserve stupid answers.*

"Well, I figured that much." She rolled her eyes and propped her fists on her hips as she stared at me.

"What was your first clue?" I snapped back at her, still frustrated I hadn't located the stamp.

"Well, I was going to ask you if you want to eat lunch with me out in the courtyard, but if you're going to be like that..."

A long sigh puffed out of my mouth. "I'm sorry, Molls. Susan just told me that Willa's check deposited into an account in the Cayman Islands, and I'm trying to figure out if the stamp we used to have that says 'For Deposit Only' with our logo is still in here somewhere."

"Oooohhhhh." Her nose scrunched up as she considered my dilemma. "I just saw that the other day when I was trying to find a rubber band."

"You did?" There had never been more hope hanging

on two words than the ones I just spoke. "The other day this week or last?"

"Probably two weeks ago." She opened the drawer of a filing cabinet that was under the counter and pulled out a plastic organizer thingamajig. It had different compartments with paper clips, rubber bands, tacks, and staples. Then she rummaged around in the back of the drawer and pulled out a cardboard box that was full of stamps.

My heart leapt as she dumped them out on the counter, and we began to hastily pick through them, examining each one and then tossing it back in the box. After looking carefully at all nine of them, we determined none was the For Deposit Only stamp. We had a Received Stamp, a couple Date Due stamps, a few with the library logo and a couple more with the address.

"I'm sure it was here, Sunshine," she said, her voice low and serious.

"Evangeline knew about that stamp," I said in a whisper.

"Do you think Jada did?"

I shrugged. "Hard to say. She's a lot newer to BBPL than the rest of us. That's an old stamp we don't use anymore. I better go tell Susan I can't find it."

Molly grabbed my hand and squeezed it. "Do you want me to come with you?"

"No, I better do it myself. I just don't understand why Evangeline would take it. It's not like her at all."

"Maybe she's being set up?" Molly shrugged. "Can we still have lunch? I'm starving!"

"Let me go talk to Susan, and I'll meet you out in the courtyard as soon as I can."

"Sounds like a plan!" My best friend smiled before scurrying off down the hallway and back toward the YA/children's area, which offered access to the courtyard.

I trudged back up the steps, my legs feeling like they weighed a million pounds apiece. Susan was typing away at a document on her computer when I arrived. I knocked on the doorframe and waited dutifully for her to admit me.

"The stamp is gone," I panted, still trying to catch my breath. Maybe all this detective work would help whip me into shape?

"Well, we might have gotten rid of it a while back," Susan speculated.

"Molly said she saw it a week or two ago when she was looking for rubber bands." I shrugged.

My boss looked at something on her computer before turning back toward me. "Listen, I need to ask you something. I have my own theories."

"Is it Jada? From Tech Services?" I guessed. "She went on vacation right after the gala, and that seems pretty suspicious to me."

Susan's nose wrinkled as she considered my suggestion. "She did?" She opened her file drawer and rifled through the folders until she came to what I assumed was Jada's personnel file. She opened it flat on her desk and began to review the various forms.

"She didn't fill out a leave request," Susan said, closing the file. "Or at least it's not in here. Now it's possible I didn't print it out, and I'll have to check my email to make sure. I'll check with my assistant too to make sure it didn't get misplaced before it went in her file."

"I wonder where she went..." I tapped my fingers on my boss's desk, a nervous habit I'd picked up from Molly. "I hope it wasn't to the Cayman Islands..."

Susan folded her hands together on top of her desk and leveled her gaze on me. "You and Evangeline are good friends, aren't you?"

My eyes widened as I stared at her, hoping beyond hope she wasn't going to accuse my friend of this heinous crime. I nodded.

"And she hasn't been at work the last two days?"

I nodded again, swallowing hard. "I've heard she's sick."

"Yessss," Susan drew out the word, "but I drove by her house this morning on my way to work, and she wasn't there."

"She wasn't?" *Oh no.* What if she was in the Cayman Islands with Jada?

"Nope." She popped the "p" on the end of the word. "I thought she liked working here," she continued. "I thought she knew how much we valued her. It's hard to believe she would betray us all like this, but I..."

"Wait," I suddenly remembered Molly said Evangeline went upstairs to the activities room to get her jacket around the time the display case was smashed. Susan was up there supervising the clean-up from dinner.

"What?" My boss's usually beady eyes rounded.

"Did Evangeline come upstairs to grab her coat while you were in the activities room on Saturday night? You know, during the announcement of our collection total, and then the Bible being stolen?"

Susan stared at me blankly for a moment like she was trying to access her memory reel from that night. And then... "No. No, I never saw her up there. After dinner, I didn't see her for the rest of the night, in fact."

Crudola.

"Okay." I heaved a sigh that came from deep within my gut, which was starting to ache like I'd been stabbed. And I had, at least figuratively. How could one of my best friends betray me like this? Betray us all?

"So you haven't talked to her about this?" Susan pressed, the slightest hint of empathy softening her sharp features. "She hasn't said anything? She wasn't behaving abnormally?"

"We'd been chatting at lunch about possible suspects," I admitted, my head now aching with the pain I'd been trying to ward off all day. "I know she called in sick, but she *never* gets sick. And Mrs. Monroe said something strange about her yesterday morning when I passed her as she was out walking her dog."

Susan's brows arched. "Willa Bryce Monroe said something about Evangeline?"

I nodded, my guts twisting as I remembered the look on the widow's face when she described my colleague as "pure evil." At this point, I didn't know what was more painful, my stomach or my head.

"What did she say?"

The thought of repeating it made me hurt even more. "Something about Evangeline being a witch...and needing the Founders' Bible for some spell or...gosh,

Susan, I don't know. The whole thing was just so...strange."

My boss's lips thinned as she stared at me, absorbing my words. "When was the last time you talked to Evangeline?"

"Tuesday." The knife in my guts twisted a little farther.

"Maybe you should pay her a visit tonight after work? And I'll look into this Jada vacation thing more closely. Maybe we can figure out what's going on."

As much as I hated to confront Evangeline, I nodded somberly. Getting to the bottom of this and recovering the money and Founders' Bible were of paramount importance. We couldn't leave any stones unturned. And if Susan thought there was a chance Evangeline could be behind the heist, I had to act on her suspicion. There was too much evidence pointing in that direction, and Susan was rarely wrong about anything.

TEN

I relayed my entire conversation with Susan as Molly drove us over to Evangeline's. We'd been friends with her for years now, but neither of us had ever been to her house. "Is that weird?" I asked Molly as she pulled into the driveway.

"I do think it's a little unusual. It's not like she said we *couldn't* come over; it's just that we always do stuff at my house or yours, or we go out."

"She doesn't like to go out," I reminded her.

"That's true. She normally doesn't come when we go out." Molly shrugged. "She's an introvert. It's not her fault."

The garage door was shut, and there was a newspaper on the porch. It was still light outside, so no telling if the lights were on inside or not. "I guess I didn't tell you what Mrs. Monroe said about our friend...?"

Molly flashed me a curious look, then launched into her own opinion on the matter, "Not sure I'd believe anything that comes out of that woman's mouth. She's not one hundred percent lucid, as far as I can tell. I talked to her for about five minutes at the gala on Saturday, and all she would do is give me advice for snatching up a man. I think it had something to do with wearing heels and cooking him his favorite dish."

I burst into laughter. "Yeah, she told me not to even bother looking for love until I lost weight, so at least your advice was a little kinder. She offered to let me borrow her diet cookbook."

"She said that?! Oh my gosh!"

I nodded, the giggles still spilling out of my mouth. It was funny, of course, but I might have been stalling. The prospect of confronting Evangeline had my stomach tangled in knots. Molly and I had both skipped dinner, thinking we'd reevaluate after we were done with this potentially unpleasant task.

I sucked in a breath as my laughter died out. "Well, she also accused Evangeline of being a witch, so..."

Molly stopped laughing and whipped around to face me. "Where are we? Salem, Massachusetts, circa the seventeenth century?"

"She said she's 'pure evil.'"

"Just because she wears black all the time and hates people?"

I shrugged. "No idea. I'm just repeating what she told me. She said Evangeline needed the Founders' Bible for some ritualistic spell or something."

"Wow, that's..." Molly shook her head and blinked rapidly, "...creative, to say the least."

"No doubt," I agreed.

Okay, we'd stalled long enough. I'd told Molly that

Susan claimed she'd driven by in the morning, but no one was home. With the garage locked up, how could she tell? Did she actually go to the door? At the time, I assumed she meant there was no car in the driveway and no garage, but now...

"C'mon, we better get going." Molly reached over to touch my hand.

I nodded, filling my lungs with an extra dose of oxygen for additional strength. *Father, please,* I prayed. *Give me the right words to say. I have no idea what I'm doing here.*

We climbed out of Molly's car and walked up the stone path to Evangeline's house. It was similar to mine, a cottage style, but hers featured gray siding and black shutters. Her living in a gray house with black shutters perfectly matched my expectations.

Molly rang the doorbell, and then we both stood there, waiting. My hand was on my hip, and Molly rocked back and forth from one foot to the other. I was surprised I couldn't hear both of our hearts pounding away. After a minute, I was almost ready to bail, but then the door handle slowly began to turn.

The sound of my blood rushing through my veins pulsed in my ears. I didn't know what I was so scared of. Was I expecting Evangeline to answer the door wielding an axe like she was about to go on a murderous rampage?

Finally, the door swung open, and Evangeline stood there looking rather like a zombie. She had a blanket wrapped around her frail shoulders, and her face was a greenish-gray color. Purple half-circles underscored her dark eyes, and her hair was unwashed and propped into a ball on top of her head in what was possibly the messiest bun in the history of messy buns. And there was that distinct odor of sickness radiating off her.

"Oh, honey!" I gasped when I saw her. She staggered back and held up her fingers in the shape of a cross. "Are you trying to tell us not to come in?"

She nodded slowly, like it was exceedingly painful to move her head even that tiny bit.

Molly spoke through the screen door, "Can we get you something? Chicken noodle soup?"

Evangeline shrugged, then shivered, wrapping the blanket tighter around her thin body. I didn't know what kind of illness she had, but I certainly didn't want to get exposed to it.

"We'll be right back." Molly lifted her index finger to indicate one minute.

Evangeline didn't even bother closing the door. She stepped back a few feet, and we saw her collapse on the sofa.

"Wow, she looks terrible!" I whispered. "Why did Susan say she wasn't home? Surely she didn't leave the house in that condition. Maybe she just didn't answer the door."

"I'm starting to understand why she didn't answer our texts," Molly said. "She looked like death warmed over!"

"Let's go get her some soup, and we'll come back. I wonder if she needs anything else." I turned back to the door and shouted through the screen, "You need anything else?"

Zombie-woman shook her head.

"Just soup?" I verified.

She gave me a weak thumbs-up. "Can you get my mail?" she added in a hoarse voice.

"Sure thing." I walked back to the car with Molly, feeling just horrible that I'd doubted my cataloguer friend. Yes, she was a bit of an odd duck, and the grumpiest person I knew—next to me, though she made me look like Miss Mary Sunshine in comparison, almost like my parents got my name right after all. But it was wrong to think, even for one second, that she could be responsible for the horrible, evil crimes that happened at the library on Saturday night. I hated the idea of her being sick, but I loved the idea of her not being a traitor!

❦

We returned to Evangeline's home about thirty minutes later with a bag of groceries and goodies for our friend. Hot chicken noodle soup from the café on the boardwalk and crackers, tissues, cough drops and a few other items to speed along her recovery.

"Hey, I'll get the mail and take these trash cans back to the house," I offered, gesturing toward the green garbage bin and the matching recycling bin with a yellow lid that were perched by the mailbox. "Can you ask our patient where they go?"

"Sure, just a sec." Molly stepped up to the porch and opened the door just wide enough to set the convalescent items inside the house. Then she turned back to me. "She says to drag them around to the back door."

That seemed like a long way to drag the trash bins

every week on garbage collection day, but whatever. There was a sidewalk that wrapped around the house, so I dragged one bin to the side of the house, dropped the mail off to Molly, who was talking to Evangeline through the door to stay as germ-free as possible, then I returned for the recycling bin.

Once I had both bins, I wheeled them around the house to where I found an enclosed deck. I froze in my tracks as a heart-stopping scene came into view.

There was an old book that looked suspiciously like the crumbling leather-bound Founders' Bible in the center of a circle of candles with an assortment of rocks, pine cones, and other nature items forming a design around it.

When my limbs finally unfroze from my initial shock, I rushed up the steps and found the screen door unlocked. I darted in, grabbed the Bible, and darted back out before evil spirits or whatever was hanging around in there could nab me. All I could hear was my blood rushing through my ears as I raced around to the front of the house, freezing again in my tracks when I saw Molly standing in the driveway, her hands on her hips.

"What's taking you so long?" she snapped. "I want to sanitize my hands!"

I realized I was clutching the Bible to my body so tightly, she couldn't even tell I was holding it. Carefully—and painstakingly slowly—I peeled the book away from my heaving chest and turned it around to show her, trying hard not to damage the fragile relic.

"Oh my gosh, is that what I think it is?" she breathed out, hardly any actual voice to her whisper.

I nodded, my whole body quivering with the realization of what this meant.

"Well, let's start by not panicking," Molly suggested as her fingers white-knuckled the steering wheel.

"Panicking? Who's panicking?" I stammered, my voice shaking with nerves.

"There has to be a reasonable explanation for this!" Molly insisted as she made the turn onto Bryce Beach's main thoroughfare.

"Besides our friend is a witch and stole our town's most prized possession for some evil sorcery?" I ran my fingers through my red curls and gave them a good tug, replacing one sting with another. "Maybe Willa was onto something!"

"Maybe she's a good witch!" Molly shrugged but kept her eyes glued to the road. "Maybe she's casting a spell to rid the town of evil spirits."

I winced. "No...no...this is all messed up. What should we do? We can't let her get away with it! Our jobs are at stake here. She cashed the checks?"

"Well, she *is* actually sick. I don't think she could fake looking that bad." Molly turned down the street where my house was. All the streets in Bryce Beach were named after flowers or trees, and I lived on Magnolia Lane.

"She's actually sick, so she's probably not going anywhere for a couple of days," I ventured. "But why in the world did she think she could get away with this?

Maybe she was going to skip town, but then came down with this bug and couldn't travel?"

"She probably didn't think anyone would come to her house and find the Bible." Molly pulled into my driveway but left her engine running. "Do you want me to come in?"

I shook my head, still clutching the Bible firmly but not too firmly. Fear that I would damage or hurt it in some way spiked the edge of every nerve in my body. I was frazzled beyond belief, and I had no idea how I was supposed to sleep tonight.

I guessed I'd broken the case. But I was not at all happy with my accomplishment. I thought I'd feel amazing when I finally figured out what happened— especially if I beat Bryce Beach PD to the punch. But I felt like a pile of poo instead.

"How could she betray us like this?"

My question floated on the air as Molly stared out the windshield. The sun was sinking into the tree line now, giving the branches an orange halo. It would be beautiful if I wasn't so upset.

My friend looked over at me with a tear glistening in her eye. *Oh no.* If she cried, I was going to cry too, and it was going to be hard to stay level-headed if I was sobbing uncontrollably.

I sucked in a deep breath. I was holding a Bible. God's Word. If anything or anyone could help me now, it was God. "I'm going to go inside, put this Bible in a safe place, and pray about it. Then I'll decide what to do."

Molly nodded. "That sounds like a good plan. I'll text you later, okay?"

"Thanks for going over there with me." When I reached over and squeezed my friend's hand, she nodded solemnly.

Then I got out of the car, cradling the Bible like a newborn as I walked up my steps and unlocked my door. I was going to figure this out. God was going to help me.

ELEVEN

F illed with a renewed strength and vigor, I got in my car on Friday morning, the Founders' Bible wrapped carefully in a towel and placed in a canvas bookbag, and drove to the Bryce Beach police station. I didn't know what the chances were that I'd be able to meet with Chief James, but I didn't want to go through the hassle of calling first and trying to get an appointment when I had such a break in the case.

I'd prayed and thought long and hard about what it meant to go to the police with this evidence and to basically throw my friend under the bus. I just kept coming back to the fact that she betrayed the library, which meant she threw all of us under the bus first.

I couldn't believe she would do that. I couldn't figure out for the life of me what her motive was. How could she witness the time and effort I put into that gala just to destroy everything I'd worked for? She knew her job was safe because she was the only cataloguer at our small library, and she had more seniority than me. She didn't have as much to worry about as I did.

I was forty-two years old, and I'd been a librarian for almost my entire life. How would I start over? Would I be forced to move away from the town my family had lived in for generations?

These were all of the fears digging their sharp claws into me when I was wrestling with how to proceed. Fortunately, my kitties had curled up next to me on the couch while I put on Netflix, and I just sat there and tried to breathe deep and relax. And then I went to the Lord and asked Him to guide me.

Reflecting back on the process I'd gone through to arrive at the conclusion I should turn Evangeline in, I parked at the station and headed inside. Though I'd lived in Bryce Beach my entire life, I'd never set foot inside the police department. I figured that was a very good thing, really, because if you have to go to the police, you're usually involved in a less-than-ideal situation.

The interior of the police station was gray and cold and looked like it had last been updated in the late eighties or early nineties. Maybe Chief James would be in a better mood if he had a more aesthetically pleasing workplace? I knew my mood improved after the library underwent its last renovation, which was about five years ago. We went from a sea of beige to vibrant beach-inspired colors like turquoise and tangerine. It was much, much better.

"Hi, I'm Sunshine Baker, and I've been working with the police on the library theft case. I have some evidence

I want to turn over to Chief James. Is he in?" I asked in my most pleasant, cheerful voice.

The receptionist gave me a bored smirk before depressing a button on her phone. "One moment."

I heard laughter bellowing down the hallway, coming from a room with an open door and a fluorescent light flooding the dim corridor. Then there was a commotion, and Chief James appeared outside the door, making eye contact with me immediately.

Just seeing him again filled me to the brim with such annoyance, I had to ask the Holy Spirit to help me tamp it down. Why did this man annoy me so much?

The receptionist looked up. "You can go to the chief's office now."

The whole exchange was weird and stiff, but at least I was getting an audience with the illustrious Chief of Police. I patted my canvas bookbag as though it was carrying the Holy Grail and traipsed down the hall toward the door the chief had just slipped into.

"Ms. Baker," he said, interlacing his fingers on his desk. "To what do I owe the pleasure?"

It was a polite thing to say, but it didn't sound polite coming from his mouth. "We found this..." I carefully set the book bag down on top of his desk, which was nearly empty save for his keyboard, monitor, and a metal file tray that contained exactly three manila folders and an interoffice mail envelope.

After he briefly examined the canvas bag, Chief James's wide, round brown eyes bore into me. "What's this?"

"It's the Founders' Bible," I said matter-of-factly.

If he was surprised, he hid it exceptionally well. He merely cleared his throat and ramped up the intensity of his gaze. "Are you sure it's the real deal?"

I scrunched up my nose as I returned his glare. "Yes, of course I am!"

I knew I shouldn't touch it because it was too fragile, but I decided to put on gloves and open it up to make sure it was the genuine article. No sense in throwing my friend under the bus if it wasn't the actual relic. The Bible was displayed open to the signatures of Nathaniel Bryce and the other founding fathers. I scoped out the signature page, and they were all there. It would be nearly impossible for someone to forge a legitimate-looking copy and make it look as old and decaying as the original.

He started to open the bag to have a look for himself, when I stopped him with a cold, hard stare. "You need to wear gloves."

You wouldn't think I'd have to say that to the Chief of Police, but...

He grunted under his breath, reached into a drawer to pull out a pair of gloves, then tugged them on. He pulled out the book, which I'd wrapped in a towel because the leather binding was so brittle and delicate that it was flaking away in parts. We'd had a preserva-tionist shore up the Bible as much as possible before we put it on display, but they couldn't make it new again, obviously.

"This looks legit," he said. "Why do you have it?"

I swallowed hard and met his penetrating stare again.

"My colleague and I found it at another colleague's house."

His back straightened in his chair as he looked back down at the Bible and then up to me again. "What colleague? What were you doing there? Why did you move it without calling us first?"

So many questions fired at me at once! A deep breath inflated my lungs as I tried to figure out how to answer. "Evangeline Dupree. She was sick, and our boss asked us to go check on her. Apparently, Susan tried to check on her yesterday morning, but she wasn't at home, which Susan found odd since Evangeline was supposedly sick."

"Go on," came his deep, baritone voice.

"So, Molly Simmons, the children's librarian, and I went to check on her last night. We got to the door, and it didn't look like she'd left for a couple of days. She looked terrible, all wrapped up in a blanket, her nose all red, and her eyes ringed with dark circles."

His lips thinned to a straight line. "Can you cut to the part where you found the Bible?"

"I'm getting to that," I snapped back, then instantly regretted taking a snarky attitude with the Chief of Police. What if he didn't believe my story and thought I stole the Bible? I was standing right next to the mayor when it happened. Who would actually believe I was behind the heist? Though I supposed some might accuse me of being an accomplice. I definitely had access to the donations too...

Wait! What am I saying?! I definitely had nothing to do with this, and if Evangeline was the guilty party, I had no clue she was involved until yesterday. That was another reason I was here. If I didn't come forward, wouldn't I be an accessory to her crime?

"We went out and got Evangeline some chicken soup; then, when we came back—we never went inside her house because, *eww*, germs... But, anyway, I got her mail and went to take her trash cans behind her house, and that's where I saw the Bible in this strange circle of candles and nature-type stuff, like it was part of some sort of, I don't know, pagan ritual!"

This actually sparked a reaction from Mr. Stone-faced. His eyes widened at the phrase "pagan ritual."

"Did you take any photographs?"

Darn it. I knew I was forgetting something important. Okay, so I had a lot to learn about detective work. "No, sir, I'm sorry. I was so...shocked to see it, I just rushed onto the porch—the door was unlocked—grabbed the Bible, I mean, carefully, of course, and then Molly and I made a quick getaway."

"And your friend never said anything about this to you before, never made you suspicious she might have been involved?" he questioned.

"No! I still have no idea why she could have wanted the Bible. I mean, the funds, okay, well, who doesn't want money?" This was the issue I kept having every time I tried to dissect this case. I just couldn't figure out where Evangeline was coming from, what her endgame was.

"Your friend has no alibi for the time when the Bible and donations went missing?" he pressed.

I thought back to what Molly said. "I was with the mayor during the commotion, but Molly said Evangeline went upstairs to get her coat from the activities room. She *did* go upstairs, but Susan claimed she didn't see her in the activities room. So it's possible she went upstairs, snuck around to the other staircase that goes to the lobby, came downstairs, smashed the glass display case, and then headed back to steal the funds from the workroom. She appeared in the crowd later."

"I see," was the only nugget of reaction Chief James would give me.

I wished I felt better about this turn of events, but the truth was, my stomach was a churning, knotted mess. I hated this conclusion. I wanted to go back and write a different ending. A happy ending.

But you couldn't argue with the evidence.

Chief James's lack of comment only made me want to keep talking. For a librarian, I was rather averse to silence, and this huge, hulking man sitting in front of me made that switch in my brain, the one that turned off my mouth when I started to ramble on, seriously malfunction.

"Of course, my initial thought was Camille Steyer stole the money, and her two little besties orchestrated the Bible theft to create a distraction for her. I even collected a hair to try to match it to a strand left at the crime scene. I interviewed Camille to see if I could glean any more evidence, and she claimed Willa Bryce Monroe had motive because she was down on her luck, and maybe she passed a bad check and wanted to cover it up by stealing the gala donations.

"So I followed up on that lead and spoke with Willa Bryce Monroe a couple days ago. Not only did she say that the Steyers were bad news and probably involved, but she also accused Evangeline Dupree of being a witch, so..." I was starting to doubt my judge of character at this point.

The chief sucked in a deep breath, moving the badge and other pins on his uniform up and back down again as he let it hiss out of his mouth slowly. "Ms. Baker, what is it you do at the library again?"

"Uh, I'm the Young Adult Librarian."

He rubbed the top of his bald head, eyes searching the ceiling for a big helping of patience, before settling his dark gaze on me again. "Why don't you stick to librarian-ship and leave the crime solving to the professionals, okay?"

I couldn't tell him that I was following my boss's orders when it came to this little sleuthing adventure. "Can you just answer one more question for me?" I pleaded. "Okay, two more questions?"

"What's that?" He sounded completely, undeniably unamused.

"Are you going to arrest Evangeline?" I felt like I should give her some notice, let her get her affairs in order before being hauled off to jail. Was I a horrible friend for giving her up on a silver platter, or was I just a good citizen who loved my town and my library? I hadn't been so conflicted since high school when I was forced to choose between 'NSync and the Backstreet Boys.

"That's none of your business," he reminded me.

I sighed. I had a feeling he wouldn't give that info up, but that didn't stop me from asking, "Susan Gooch said that at least one of the stolen checks from the gala was deposited into an account in the Cayman Islands."

His lips thinned, nostrils flaring as he surveyed me, but he didn't respond.

"Do you know if the check was stamped with a 'For Deposit Only' stamp and the library's logo on the back? Do you know the name on the account?"

"Librarianship, Ms. Baker. That's your wheelhouse. Leave this investigation to the pros. Now, I need to get back to work. Have a pleasant day." He stood up, scooting his chair loud enough to make a horrible grinding noise against the gray tile floor.

He tried to pull the top manila file folder off the stack on his metal tray as I stood up to leave, but I inadvertently bumped the corner of the tray with my hip and sent it crashing to the floor right at my feet. My face flushed with embarrassment as something like a growl rumbled out of his mouth.

"I'm so sorry!" I bent down to retrieve the files, and the top one had fallen opened. It was clearly related to our Bryce Beach Bandit case. The printout was from a bank account in the Cayman Islands, and it had the bank logo at the top. I was just getting ready to take a mental photograph of the account holder's name when Chief James stepped around the desk and tapped me on the shoulder.

"Hand it over," he barked.

Before I could fully absorb the logo or the name, I had to surrender the evidence. I left his office as fast as my feet could carry me, my fingers trembling at losing my chance to discover where the library's money had gone.

TWELVE

I snuck in the back door at work, hoping no one would notice I'd come in so late. When I made it to the YA area, across the room from the children's area, Molly looked like she was about to combust, bouncing up and down in her chair with suspense.

I lifted a finger in the air when my phone rang. It was Susan's line, so I knew I needed to answer it. "Yes?"

"What happened when you went to check on Evangeline last night?" she demanded without any semblance of a preamble.

I was already feeling on edge after my meeting with Chief James, but now my nervous system was really revved up. Jitters danced up and down my limbs like I was the victim of caffeine overload, when I had, in fact, only guzzled down a mere two cups.

"Uh, she's actually sick," I answered, which was the whole truth and nothing but the truth. "We didn't go inside because she looked so awful, and whatever she has looked like something neither of us wanted to catch. We went out and got her some chicken noodle soup and brought it back to her."

"Oh," was all my boss said. And then after a few beats, she asked, "You didn't go inside her house at all then?"

"No, ma'am, didn't want to run the risk of picking up any of her germs."

"Aren't you forgetting a detail or two?" she pressed, her voice full of suspicion.

My mind raced as I wondered how she would know about the Bible we found.

"Chief James just called me," she said. "I know you found the Bible over there."

"Oh..." I scrambled for an explanation. "Sorry, I didn't know if I was allowed to speak to that."

"It's my library, Baker!" she roared. "Everything that happens here is my business. And I told you to be the eyes and ears of this case!"

Earlier in the week, she was devastated and crying. I guessed the anger stage had kicked in, because she sure was fuming now. *What a difference a few days makes!*

When I didn't respond, her tone softened. "I'm sorry, I didn't mean to yell at you. I just wanted you to know you did the right thing. I know you and Evangeline are friends, but there's too much at stake here, and you don't want to be an accessory to a crime, right?"

"No, of course not!"

"Well, let's just hope the police can recover the money from that account," she said. "The library's days are numbered if we don't get our hands on those donations."

The ominous tone of her voice clanged in my ears like a gong as I hung up the phone and lifted my gaze to Molly, who was about to come unglued as she watched my conversation from across the room.

The floor was empty, no patrons in sight in our area, and Tom was occupied with helping a patron at one of the computers across from the circulation desk. I raced over to Molly's desk.

"Well?!" she burst out as though the words were rocket-fueled.

"The chief already called Susan to tell her about the Bible. He told me to quit playing amateur detective." I rolled my eyes as Molly scoffed.

"You were only doing what Susan asked you to do!"

"I know!" I retorted. "He told me to stick to librarian-ship and leave the detective work to the professionals."

"Whatever. You'd think he would at least thank you for recovering the Bible. That's more than his detectives did!"

"Thank you! You're right!" I vigorously nodded. He never once said thank you or showed any gratitude for my help at all.

"I mean, you basically solved his whole case and delivered it to him on a silver platter," Molly continued.

"No kidding." Now I was even more annoyed than I was earlier today when I met with him. The nerve of that guy to not even say thank you. "He's just jealous I did a better job at his job than he did."

Molly let out a breath as she slumped in the chair behind her desk. "Wow, I can't believe it's over." Her shoulders sagged as she lifted her pale blue eyes to me.

Her words sank in, leaving me with a similarly deflated feeling. "It is, isn't it?"

"We're going to get the Bible back, and it's only a matter of time until they arrest Evangeline and they're able to access her account."

"Will they be able to, though? If it's in a foreign country?"

"I don't know exactly how it works," Molly admitted. "But you know who would?"

I was almost afraid to hear her answer. "Who?"

She glanced over at Tom, who had finished helping the patron and was strolling back to his desk.

"Oh, no. No thank you. The last time I talked to him, I got an earful about an amphibious World War II tank."

Molly laughed. "Well, he'd know the answer; I'm sure of it. I imagine they can recover the money, but it's going to take some time."

"As long as we get it, that's all that matters." Even though I still felt sick about Evangeline's betrayal, I did feel like a huge burden had been lifted from my chest. I hopefully wouldn't be losing my job.

My friend patted me on the back. "Well, nice job solving the mystery!"

"You helped! I couldn't have done it without you." I wanted to celebrate, but knowing Evangeline had duped us all left a big, gaping hole right in the middle of my heart.

Spotting the defeated look on Molly's face, I had an inkling she felt the exact same way. "Maybe we could go walk on the beach tonight? Stop by The Candy Shoppe to pick up a little something?"

"Are we celebrating or commiserating?" I sighed.

She tilted her head thoughtfully. "I think a little of both."

B risk spring air, the smell of the sea air, and fresh fudge were rather therapeutic, if I said so myself. My best friend and I walked along the surf with our sandals dangling by our index fingers as chilly waves rushed up around our feet and ankles. My toes were numb by the time we made it back to the boardwalk, but I didn't even care. The chilling effect seemed to soothe my soul, which was in tatters after learning the third member of our librarian trifecta had betrayed us.

I was saying goodbye to Molly and walking back to my car when my phone rang. I didn't recognize the number, but it was local, so I took a chance and answered it. "Hello?"

"Call from Bryce Beach City Jail. Do you accept?" came a static female voice that sounded like a recording. "Press 'one' for yes, 'two' for no, and 'zero' for the operator."

I had a bad feeling about this but pressed "one" anyway. "Hello?"

"Sunshine!" came a desperate plea on the other end. "Sunshine, you have to come down here right now!"

"Evangeline?" I'd never heard her sound so out-of-sorts before, though I supposed being tossed in the slammer would have that effect on you. I was surprised she wanted anything to do with me if she figured out

Molly and I were the ones to make the discovery on her patio.

"Please," she said, "I'm begging you. Tell them I didn't steal the Bible. Tell them I'm not a witch. Please! You know I would never do anything like that. They set the bail very high, Sunshine. I don't know what to do. I don't have any family around here, and no one to help me. Can you please come down here?"

An anguished wail sounded down the line, and I felt like my heart was being ripped in two. *Oh, Lord, what do I do?* I prayed, hoping an answer would become clear as soon as I filled my lungs with air and let it out again slowly.

"I'll come down there," I decided, "but I don't know if there's anything I can do to help. Evangeline, Molly and I found the Bible at your house last night when we were there."

"I know," she answered. "But I didn't put it there. Please, you have to believe me! Please help me. You know I couldn't have done anything like that. I could never put money in an account in the Cayman Islands. You know how much I hate the Caribbean and anything to do with sun or beach or sand. Cayman Islands? No freaking thank you! I would have put it someplace cool, both in temperature and hipness. Sunshine, c'mon, you have to believe me!"

I sighed yet again, trying to figure out if it mattered if I believed her. The important thing now was the evidence. If we ever got it back, I needed to convince Susan to spend some of the donation money on security cameras. Security cameras would have cleared this whole mess up or prevented it from happening in the first place.

"I'll come down there," I repeated myself, "but I don't know if there is anything I can do to help."

"You have to try," she begged. "Please promise me you'll try..."

I closed my eyes and let the promise float off my tongue: "I'll try."

T he city jail was conveniently attached to the police station, so I made my second trip of the day there. Molly had already headed off to her car, and I thought about letting her know Evangeline had called, but I decided this was something I should do alone. I whipped into a parking space and rushed inside.

Fortunately, it was a different receptionist than the blasé woman I'd dealt with earlier in the day. This character looked like a rookie cop. He was young and had a pencil-thin moustache.

"Hi, I'm here to see Evangeline Dupree at the jail," I announced.

Judging by the scowl on his face, he wasn't much friendlier than his predecessor. "You want to head down that hallway, hit the intercom to be buzzed in, and then there's a desk you can check in at."

"Okay, thank you." I marched down the hallway, my stomach twisting into knots, but I felt a pull, something urging me on, giving me energy. I didn't know if it was the hand of God or if it was the sugar from the fudge I'd eaten with Molly. Maybe a combination of both.

I checked in at the table, delivering the same spiel I'd given the young cop. This one was much older and heavier, with a silvery-gray five o'clock shadow and beady brown eyes that were barely visible behind the thick lenses of his glasses.

"Are you here to bail Ms. Dupree out?" he questioned, glancing down at her paperwork. I couldn't believe so much was still done by paper here instead of computer. And I thought we were Luddites at the library!

"Uh..." She didn't ask me to bail her out, only to come speak with her. "I just wanted to talk to her."

He shook his head. "Visitation hours are tomorrow from nine to noon. I can only release her now if her bail is paid."

"How much is it?"

"Twenty thousand," he announced.

Twenty thousand? My heart sank. Like I had that kind of cash lying around! "I guess I'll have to come back in the morning, then."

"You do that," was all he said.

Why was everyone here so rude? It was almost like they were used to dealing with brazen, hardened criminals who had no respect for authority or something.

I headed home, anxious to see my handsome boy, Bond, and my baby girl, Paigie-Poo. They'd be a sight for sore eyes. And a damaged heart.

THIRTEEN

My phone rang at 7:23 AM. My mother. Evidently, 7:23 was the official time it became acceptable to call someone. At least if you gave birth to that someone.

"Hey, Mom..." I was too groggy to put together anything more intelligent than that. I'd had a restless, fitful night, and I was pretty sure the masked person wielding a knife and chasing me in my dreams was Evangeline. She was a little bit scary before I found out she was a thief and possibly a witch, but in the dream she was downright terrifying.

"Morning, sweetheart, I just wondered if you saw *The Bryce Beach Gazette* this morning?"

"Mom, I'm still in bed. I haven't seen anything but the back of my eyelids."

"Oh, well, you made the front page!" she gushed.

I leapt out of bed. Apparently, if I ever needed an alternative to an alarm clock, the words "You made the front page" would do rather nicely. My heart was pounding so fast, it was like I'd either chugged a gallon of coffee, or I'd sprinted around the house like the cats do when they're momentarily possessed.

"Sweetheart, are you okay?" my mother continued when she didn't hear any response from me. My mind was racing too fast to latch on to any specific thought. "You're not in any kind of trouble, are you?"

"Trouble?" I repeated, the images from the nightmares that plagued me the night before popping up in my head.

"Well, the woman they arrested is your friend Evangeline, isn't it? You turned her in?"

Thanks for reminding me, Mom.

"Yeah, uh, Molly and I found the Founders' Bible at her house." By this time, I had pulled up the news story on my laptop. They used a photo of the Founders' Bible from when it was still in its case, not a photo of me. *Thank you, Lord!* There wasn't a photo of Evangeline either, and for that I was also grateful. Though I supposed a person like Evangeline didn't have a lot of photos floating around. She didn't do social media.

I scanned the article quickly while my mother blathered on about doing the right thing and how she and my dad were proud of me. At least that was something they could agree on.

"Mom, I have to go. I'm sorry..."

"You're sure you're not in trouble?"

"Yes, Mom, I'm sure. Just need to get ready for work."

And to stop by jail, no biggie.

"Your nephews have a Little League game this afternoon at four. Any chance you can stop by? It would mean a lot to River and Izzy. And we could all go out for pizza afterwards!" she tried to tempt me.

"I'll try to stop by, Mom," I promised.

I felt guilty after I hung up that I was in such a foul mood, but ever since I'd found that Bible, I'd felt like a miserable failure. I felt betrayed, like I'd been duped, and like I should have protected the donations better than I did. I was in charge of them, after all!

And then there was Evangeline...

I was going to stop by and see her this morning during visiting hours because I said I would. I hoped she hired a lawyer...

❀

I didn't like the fact that my cute little red Mazda was getting so accustomed to driving to the police depart- ment. *It's still early May*, I reminded myself. Summer was coming, and hopefully by the time it got here, this whole Bryce Beach Bandit incident would be behind us. The library would get our money; I could order some new books; I'd have job security—and I'd never have to play amateur sleuth again. I could "stick to librarianship," just like Chief James suggested.

I checked in at the jail wing of the building and sat on a plastic chair—gray, like everything else in the joint— until my name was called. A tall, muscular female guard patted me down and made me put my purse and cell phone in a plastic bin. "I'll return it when you leave," she told me.

I nodded and followed her down a dismally gray

hallway until we came to a small room with a door that had a glass window at eye level. Evangeline was sitting inside with her hands cuffed together, wearing a pair of gray sweatpants and a white shirt. She would never, ever choose to wear white. She probably hated that more than the cuffs.

The guard showed me inside, and Evangeline barely even looked up to acknowledge me. How was I going to explain why I did what I did?

"Are you feeling better?" I remembered how ill she'd been when I last saw her, and she finally turned toward me. She looked better than she had the other night at her house, but still not well. Her skin was always sallow and pale, and she always had dark circles under her eyes, but at least her nose wasn't bright scarlet this time, and her eyes didn't look as listless and dull. It was an improvement.

"I might feel better if I weren't in here," she snapped.

Her dark eyes finally met mine and were so full of pain, I winced. "I'm so sorry..."

"I didn't do it, Sunshine." She leaned toward me, her eyes bouncing between mine as she implored, "You have to figure out who really did it. I was framed. I had no idea that book was on my patio. I swear."

I had a feeling she was going to say that. "Do you have any idea who could have put it there?"

She shook her head. "No. I was so sick the last couple of days, I couldn't even get out of bed. That's why I didn't answer your texts. I wasn't ignoring you. I was so glad when you guys dropped by—I hadn't seen or talked to anyone since the last day I was at work. I don't even know what day that was now. I have absolutely no idea why whoever stole the Bible—and I guess the money too—is trying to frame me, of all people. And they're claiming I'm a witch? I may be goth or emo, but I'm no witch!"

I remembered how Molly reported that Evangeline went upstairs to get her jacket just prior to the mayor's announcement, so she was gone when the Bible was actually stolen. And then I recalled how Susan claimed she never saw Evangeline come into the room to get the jacket. Molly said Evangeline hadn't even been wearing a jacket that night, which was pretty incriminating. Wasn't it?

"Let me ask you something, okay?" I folded my arms over my chest to show I meant business. "I need you to be one hundred percent honest, or I can't help you."

"Anything. I promise." She sucked in a deep breath, her small frame rising and falling as she inhaled and exhaled.

"First off…" I tried to figure out the best way to phrase it so I could catch her if she were lying. "Have you ever used a stamp with the library's logo on it?"

Her brows drew together. "Stamp? What kind of stamp?"

"You tell me." I waited for recognition to flash across her eyes and for her to deny it.

"The tech services folks who process the books after I catalog them stamp Bryce Beach Public Library on the edges of the pages," she admitted. "But I never do it myself. I always get ink on my hands when I use one of those stupid inkpads." A little laugh fluttered out of her mouth.

The ink on those pads was potent stuff, I could agree there. No matter how hard you scrubbed, it usually took a few days to wear off. I always got ink on myself too because I was a klutz like that. I looked down at Evangeline's hands, which were cuffed at the wrist. "Let me see your hands."

She bit her bottom lip and held them out, palms up at first, and then she turned them over. It had been almost a week since the heist, but the checks weren't deposited until Tuesday, so there could still be a trace of ink on them, I supposed. But I didn't see anything, not even a faint stain.

"Why are you asking me about stamps?"

I ignored her. "I have another question for you."

"Okay?"

"Where were you when the glass case was shattered?" I asked point-blank, then I tuned in to watch her reaction, taking note of each tiny muscle movement around her eyes and mouth as I searched for signs she was lying.

She narrowed her eyes for a moment, then pursed her lips as if she needed to think about it. I could tell the moment it clicked because her whole face brightened, and when Evangeline's face brightened, it was very noticeable because it was not part of her typical facial expression repertoire.

"I was standing there with Molly—you'd just gone to give the mayor the final tally of donations. I thought we would be leaving right after the announcement, but then I remembered I left my jacket upstairs. I thought I'd taken it off at dinner and hung it on the back of my chair. So I told Molly I was going upstairs to get it."

"And?" I drilled into her with my cold, hard stare of pure business, knowing full well she wasn't even wearing a jacket the whole night.

Her eyes stayed locked onto mine, never wavering. "So, I got upstairs to the activities room and started to look around the table where I'd sat, but then I realized it wasn't there."

"It wasn't?"

"No. And it was only then that I realized I left it in the car. I was wearing a sweater over my dress, and I was hot in my car, so I left it out there." She smirked at her memory. "So, it was a wasted trip."

"What else do you remember seeing in the activities room?" I delved a little deeper.

Her eyes took on a faraway look as she examined her memories of the night, then she fluttered back into reality, a look of confusion twisting her features. "I didn't think much of it at the time, or maybe I just forgot, because as soon as I got back downstairs, I saw everyone gathered around the lobby and all the broken glass. And the screams. Ouch, I can still hear the screams in my ears."

"What did you see, Evangeline?"

"Well, when I came up to the top of the stairs to head into the activities room, Susan was rushing out. I tried to stop her to thank her for the candy she'd given me after the dinner. It really got the fish taste out of my mouth. But she brushed past me, almost knocking me down, and she didn't even say she was sorry. I watched her for a second because it seemed like something was wrong—she was on a mission. She didn't go down the main stairs..."

Evangeline's eyes widened as she started to realize where my line of questioning was going.

"Where did she go?"

"She disappeared into the stacks toward the front of the building," my friend relayed. "And I just remembered something else... She was wearing gloves, Sunshine..."

A little burst of air puffed out of my mouth when it all started to click. "Could she have gone down the front steps into the lobby?"

"Yes," Evangeline agreed. "At the time, I thought she was wearing gloves because she was helping the caterers clean up..."

"Right, that makes sense. Could she have been in the lobby without anyone noticing her?"

"Definitely. I heard the cheer from the mayor's announcement clear up in the activities room. Then the DJ started up 'Celebration' by Kool & the Gang, and she certainly had to be down the stairs by then, if that's where she was going. I looked around the room for a few minutes before I realized I'd left my jacket in the car, then, when I got to the stairs—the main ones—that's when I heard screams and saw everyone moving toward the lobby as I flew down the stairs to join them." She scrubbed her hand down her face. "I should have followed Susan instead..."

"I can't believe it!" I gasped. "It was our boss!"

"We need proof," Evangeline rushed out. "Something to exonerate me and prove it was her."

At that moment, the visual I snapped of the account

statement in the file folder on Chief James's desk flashed into my mind. I still couldn't say for sure what the bank logo was or determine the name on the account, but I did have the most amazing idea of all time.

"I have an idea," I announced, standing up.

"Wait! Tell me your plan!" Evangeline begged as I rushed toward the door. "I'm sorry I'm just now putting two and two together. I would have never suspected in a million years—"

"Sit tight. I'll be back for you as soon as I can!" I promised, and with that, I bolted down the hall, retrieved my purse and phone from the guard, and raced to my car.

"To the library!" I exclaimed to no one in particular as I fired up my Mazda. I had work to do!

FOURTEEN

Molly was doing another story time with preschoolers when I arrived at work, so I couldn't update her on my chat with Evangeline. My fingers trembled as I pulled up the email I'd received from Anna Cooper's sister, Liz, with her resume. She indeed won a cyber hacking contest last summer. I didn't even know there was such a thing, but it certainly served my purposes.

I dialed her number, knowing full well she would be in school. It was ten o'clock on Friday morning, after all. To my great surprise, she answered.

"Elizabeth Cooper?" my voice vibrated with nervous energy. Even though I kept coaching myself to remain calm, I was scared that the longer I waited to gather the evidence I needed, the more likely it was that the true culprit would get off scot-free.

"Who's calling please?" the young lady asked in a polite but wary voice.

"This is Sunshine Baker, the YA Librarian at the public library. I received your resume earlier this week, and I actually have a very urgent job for you, if you're interested." I cleared my throat. "Aren't you supposed to be in school right now?"

"I'm in gym class. We're supposed to be jogging on the track, but I'm participating in an...um...alternative activity."

"Alternative activity?"

"Walking and talking on the phone," she clarified.

This was a girl after my own heart, just like her sister.

"Do you think you could stop by after school to help me with a project?" I queried, crossing my fingers she would say yes. Time was of the essence.

"Yeah, I can do that. What's the job pay? How many hours do you need me?"

Crud. I hadn't thought that far in advance. "Um... twenty dollars an hour?" That was a lot for a high school student, wasn't it? "Hopefully it won't take long at all. You're a hacker, right?"

"You want me to hack something?" She couldn't disguise the excitement in her voice.

"Uh, I'm not going to do anything unethical with the information, I promise. I just need to see who owns an account at a bank in the Cayman Islands."

"Oh," she said, just that one staccato word. For a second I thought she was going to tell me no, she wasn't interested. But then: "As long as it's for a good cause."

My heart fluttered with hope. "Oh, trust me, it's for a *very* good cause."

"I'll see you at three, then," she said matter-of-factly. And then she hung up. She was businesslike—not what I expected from a sixteen-year-old, but if she had the kind of skills I thought she did, she could be rude and have terrible hygiene, and I wouldn't care. Though I couldn't imagine either of those being the case based on what I knew of her family.

I looked up, and standing right there in front of me was my boss.

"Who were you talking to?" she demanded, a scowl deepening the lines on her face.

"Oh, just a patron," I fibbed. *Also for a good cause!* "She's coming in this afternoon to pick up a book I have on hold for her."

"Aren't all your patrons in school right now?" She flashed a wicked smirk, like she'd caught me in a treacherous lie. *Which I suppose she did.*

"She was on a break," I explained. "I thought I'd be leaving a voicemail, but she actually answered." A nervous smile spread across my face. "I got lucky!"

"Did you hear about Evangeline?" my boss changed the subject.

My heart was beating in my ears. Susan didn't normally come down to the YA or children's area unless she wanted something specific. Maybe she was planning to sit in on Molly's story time?

"I did." I glanced over to the large round rug where Molly always read to the children, wondering how much longer story time would go on. There were a few fidgety preschoolers, one of whom had given up on the story and was wandering around the toy area, picking up toys and then tossing them back on the ground.

What if she's down here to fire me? the thought blazed through my head. She couldn't fire me before I could bring her down!

Susan's hands migrated to her hips. "Well, let's hope they can recover those donations so no one loses their job. Except Evangeline, of course. She's not coming back."

I shook my head. I didn't suppose she would be—not until after I could prove Susan was behind all of this and framed Evangeline. Once again, I wished I had some spy gadgets. If I could have bugged her phone or office, or put a tracker on her car—

Susan's cell phone rang, and I didn't know if it was saving me or just adding another steep drop-off to this roller coaster we were riding. She turned away from me and slid the phone to her ear. "Hello? Oh, hi, Chief!"

She said that loud enough that I could hear, but then her voice dipped. It sounded like mostly "okays" and "mmhmmms," and then she turned around to face me. "Of course we're ready to take the Founders' Bible back as soon as possible. I can have a new display case delivered immediately."

She threw her head back and laughed. "Well, we will have a new security system installed as soon as the donations are returned to us. Thanks, Chief."

An evil grin spread across her face as she slid her phone back into her pocket. "It's all coming together."

With that, I couldn't tell if she knew that I knew she was the mastermind, or if she was operating under the assumption I still thought Evangeline was the culprit. I noticed Molly finishing up the story and chatting with a few parents as they prepared to whisk their little tykes back out into the beautiful spring weather. I shot her a look that said, "Get over here ASAP," or at least I hoped she would interpret it as such.

"Chief James did say something interesting, though," Susan said, drawing my eyes back to her.

"Oh?" I hoped to stall long enough for Molly to make it over to join in our discussion. She was shifting her weight from foot to foot while she tried to escape a conversation with a mom who was practically getting dragged away by a very insistent and apparently very strong-willed three-year-old.

"Yes, he said more checks were deposited into that Cayman Islands account yesterday." She scratched her chin and leveled her gaze on me.

Molly rushed to my side just as I responded, "But Evangeline couldn't have done that from jail."

"Exactly." Susan acknowledged Molly's arrival with a slight nod. "That means she must have an accomplice."

I looked over just in time to see the curiosity flicker across my friend's face. She still didn't know what I'd discovered this morning when I spoke with Evangeline. She was way behind, and I'd have to figure out how to update her without Susan finding out. What if she had this whole place bugged? I wouldn't put it past her if she was willing to frame her own employees and steal money from the library.

"I believe you were onto something the other day when you mentioned Jada from Tech Services," our boss said. "I want you and Molly here to pay her a visit this afternoon and find out if she's involved. You did such a great job proving Evangeline stole the Bible... How much do you want to bet you'll find the missing cash or the rest of the stolen checks at Jada's place? Maybe even that stamp you were looking for, Sunshine?"

Molly flashed me a questioning look, but I decided to play along. Hopefully by this afternoon I'd have my evidence against Susan with the help of teen hacker extraordinaire, Liz Cooper. And if I was wrong, at least I'd know who the account in the Cayman Islands belonged to, and we could go from there. Maybe it was Jada and Evangeline working together, but I bet a burnt batch of biscuits it was Susan.

"I have a meeting at three, and then we'll head over there," I told our boss. "But I thought Jada was on vacation?"

"Oh, she returned last night, actually. She was due in today, but she called in sick. Though now I'm starting to wonder if she went anywhere at all." Susan rolled her eyes.

There was certainly a lot of illness going around. Did she have the same thing Evangeline had? "I guess we'll find out!" I vowed.

"Excellent. Thank you both for all your hard work. I will be rewarding your loyalty when it comes to review time!" she promised with a satisfied smile, then she turned and headed up the stairs to her cushy lair... er...office.

"What the flim-flam is going on?" Molly's eyes

doubled in size as soon as we were alone. "Did you see Evangeline?"

"Come on," I took her hand, "we've gotta go outside. I'm afraid this place is..." I glanced around the floor, hoping she'd pick up on my stellar context clues. "Grab your lunch."

Her brows furrowed as she slowly nodded, went over to her desk to retrieve her lunch bag, and followed me out into the courtyard. It was almost time for lunch anyway, so no one would think it was strange that we were going outside.

I filled her in on what happened when I saw Evangeline this morning, and I thought her eyes might just pop right out of her head, they'd grown so large. "So now what?"

I took a deep breath and launched into my plan: "Liz Cooper, Anna Cooper's older sister, is coming by after school to help me track down the name on the account where the funds were deposited. Do you think you could go over to Jada's on your own, just to appease Susan? Maybe you can warn her about what's going on—if she's even there. I'm guessing Susan is going to plant the checks and deposit only stamp over there, if she hasn't already. She's probably waiting for both Jada and Evangeline to be in jail, poised to take the rap, and then she'll get the heck out of Dodge."

"How in the world will you find the account?" Molly squinted at me in disbelief. "That sounds like finding a needle in a haystack."

"Liz is a hacker, Molls. She won a hacking competition a couple of years ago, and that means she's only gotten more skilled since then. We're going to figure out which bank it is, and then we're going to search deposits from the last few days. I think I'll know the bank when I see it—and the deposits, at least Mrs. Monroe's. I have a photographic memory, and I saw part of the account name in the file I knocked off Chief James's desk."

"I still don't know how you're going to pull this off!" she gasped, seemingly amused by my naivete. "How will you know you've got the right bank?"

"I'll recognize the logo when I see it. It was blue and had a white palm tree."

"You sound pretty confident." I couldn't tell if her statement was a compliment or a criticism.

"I am. You'll see." I couldn't explain why I was so sure my plan would work, but I was. Maybe it was some sort of divine help, or maybe I was just meant to solve this mystery. Either way, I was going to get to the bottom of this, and the library would be saved. I was going to prove Chief James wrong too—I could be an amazing librarian AND an amazing detective!

"Alright. I guess I'm along for the ride," Molly said, still not sounding totally convinced. "But why do we have to go see Jada? Do you think she's sick with what Evangeline had?"

"If Susan is behind all this, that means she planted the Bible at Evangeline's house. She's likely planted some other evidence, probably the checks and the deposit only stamp, to implicate Jada. If you can find it when you're there, we'll be a step ahead of the police, and maybe we can help keep Jada from getting arrested PLUS use the evidence against Susan." I was talking so fast, I could tell my friend was having a hard time keeping up.

"I still think you're nuts, and this could all come crashing down on us, but I'll try to keep an open mind. Are you sure you can't just go with me?" Molly pleaded.

I tried to find the right words to convince my best friend this was the best plan. "I want to make sure I get the info I need from Liz, and I don't want to rush her. If I get the answer I expect, I'm going straight to see Chief James—hopefully I can get there before Susan has a chance to skip town. Then I'm supposed to stop by the Little League diamond to see my nephews play baseball at four, so there's a bit of a time crunch."

"Okay," she conceded, but trepidation still clouded her pale blue eyes. "I wish I felt as sure about this as you do... I just feel like something could go wrong."

"Are you scared of Susan?" I asked her point-blank.

She shrugged. "She's been acting weird, and look at what she's already done. It's crazy, isn't it? Aren't you a little leery?"

I scoffed. "You can't scare me. I voluntarily work with teens."

A smile cracked her lips. "Good point."

⁂

At 3:15, Anna and her sister strolled through the door. I would have known it was Anna's sister even if the two weren't together. She was a little taller and heavier than Anna, but they had the same hairline, same tawny-colored complexion, same flare to their nostrils, and the same beautiful smile.

"Elizabeth?" I asked as the two approached my desk.

"You can call me Liz," she said with a grin that matched her sister's. "Nice to meet you, Ms. Baker."

"Likewise." I shook her hand, then cut to the chase. "Okay, so here's what I need." I gestured to the bank of computers on the edge of the YA section. Sometimes my patrons came in and worked on school papers at these stations, but otherwise they didn't get much use other than quick internet searches and games.

Liz sat down, and I logged her in using the generic library guest username and password. I told her I was looking for a bank in the Cayman Islands that had a blue logo with a white palm tree, and she cracked her knuckles and went right to Google.

"I'm pretty sure you could have done that search yourself, Ms. Baker," Anna pointed out as she stood looking over her sister's shoulder.

"After we find the right bank, that's when I really need your skills," I explained. "Consider this a warm-up drill."

"Gotcha." Liz's fingers began to fly over the keys.

I looked over and saw Molly gathering up her purse and lunch bag. She was on her way to Jada's to warn her about what was going on—if she was even there, of course. I would go straight to the police if Liz's hacking came through, and Molly would meet me there if she found anything of interest at Jada's.

"Is this it?" came Liz's voice from the computer, and

when I looked over at the screen, the logo I saw on the paperwork in the file jumped out at me.

I gasped. "That's it!"

"Great. Now what do you need to know?"

Over the course of the past couple days, the donors had supplied us with a list of the checks they'd written. We sheepishly emailed everyone on our newsletter subscription list and confessed the funds had been stolen, and we needed help tracking them down. Of course, everyone in town already knew that, but it stung to admit it to our most ardent supporters.

After I handed over the list of deposit amounts, Liz studied it carefully. "Just find the deposits?"

"I know for sure the check for twenty grand was deposited earlier this week. I need to know the name on the account it was deposited into," I explained.

I had no sooner fired the words off my tongue than I heard a gasp fly out of Molly's mouth. When I looked up, Susan was coming down the stairs with a murderous glare in her beady dark eyes. *Oh no.*

Pretending nothing was awry—*and doing a darn good job of it, I might add*—I walked over to Molly and asked her if she was ready. She nodded slowly, but I saw the look of fear etched deep in her features.

"Are you going now?" I whispered.

She pumped her head up and down just as Susan made her way into the space between the YA area and the children's area. "Shouldn't you two be leaving together?" our boss demanded.

My heart set off at a fast trot as I looked toward Liz, whose screen was facing away from Susan, thank the

Lord. "Oh, I'm just helping Anna and Liz here. I was going to let Molly go ahead without me so I can finish up here and run a couple of other errands."

Anna seemed to sense what was going on and came to my rescue. "After Liz is done with her project, I need help finding sources for my English paper. It's on *Romeo and Juliet*," she improvised.

I love that girl! My heart swelled with pride as my gaze bounced between my boss and my best friend.

"I'll be fine without Sunshine," Molly insisted.

Susan's jaw clenched. "I'm just thinking your mission would be more successful if you both went, you know? You make such a good team. Just look at what you uncovered the other night? It was the break in the case the police needed."

I looked over to Liz, who was furiously typing away, her focus completely absorbed in what she was doing. Anna stood behind her, looking protective, as if she understood we needed to keep the project a secret from the library director.

"How about this? I'll finish up here with Liz and Anna, and I'll meet Molly over there when I'm done," I suggested. Why was she so insistent we go together? She was acting so weird!

Molly knew I needed time to get over to the police station before dropping by my nephews' baseball game. "I was just on my way now." She gestured to her purse slung over her shoulder. "It's fine for Sunshine to catch up later. Maybe I'll stop off for coffee or something first. I could use a pick-me-up."

She sounded surprisingly nonchalant for what was

going on—I was so impressed with her acting skills! My eyes snapped to my boss, hoping she would buy it. That was the true test.

"Okay," Susan relented. "Just call me if you need backup or anything."

Molly smiled. "I'm sure I'll be fine."

As Susan was walking back up the stairs, Liz's eyes popped up over the screen. "Found it."

FIFTEEN

I stared at the screen for several seconds, trying to make sense of the dazzling lines of white text against a black background. "What am I even looking at?"

"These are the transactions the bank has processed since Monday," Liz answered, scrolling down the lines of text. "I did a search for twenty thousand, and these are the ones that came up." She highlighted the top ten lines.

"Can you see the account names?"

Liz moved the cursor over to the list of names, and I scanned through them:

William Beech...nope
Stanley LaPierre...no
Gloria Fenwick...probably not
Leslie McCain...nuh uh
Sandra Whitehead...nope
Travis Elliott-Pence...sigh
Eleanor Gibson...I don't think so

> *Harold Xu...not a chance*
> *Victor Lopez...'fraid not*
> *Gus Schoona...negative, Ghostrider*

"No luck?" Anna asked, and when I lifted my eyes to meet hers, I lost my place in the lines of text.

"I probably shouldn't have expected it to be her name. I mean, she isn't stupid. She doesn't want it connected to her. She probably made up an alias..."

I scanned the female names again to see if any of them sounded like something Susan Gooch, a sixty-something-year-old library director from a small town on the East Coast would make up. Somebody who liked crossword puzzles and mysteries. Somebody who owned cats and tons of books and knew how to knit—though librarians were contractually obligated to do those things, as far as I knew. Someone who made the best darn Buffalo chicken dip I'd ever eaten.

And then...

Then, like the Lord sent an angel to paint a picture inside my head, I got a very clear mental image of the book that was sticking out of Susan's bookcase when I was in there earlier this week: *Anagrams, Crosswords, and Word Games.*

"It's an anagram!" I shouted, so loud that one of Tom's patrons across the aisle shot me a nasty look.

I scanned the list again, my eyes falling on the very last one: *Gus Schoona.*

It was an anagram of *Susan Gooch.*

"Can you get inside that account?" I pointed to Gus on the screen.

"Let me see." Liz's fingers moved like lightning on the keys, and before I knew it, another list of transactions appeared, the ones in Gus Schoona's account.

$20,000

$500

$300

$1500

$250

"That's it!" I squealed. "We did it! Those are donation amounts; I just know it. And when they actually look at the checks, I bet you anything they were made out to Bryce Beach Public Library and are stamped 'For Deposit Only' with our logo on the back. There's no way you can hack in to see images, is there?"

"Sure, I can try. They're probably stored on a different server." Liz shrugged and turned back to the computer like this was the easiest job in the world.

"Wait, print out that transaction list for me, okay? I'm going to go take this to the police, and then if you're able to see the actual checks, print those out and call me, okay?"

Liz was typing so fast and was so engrossed, she didn't even hear me, but Anna wore a huge grin on her face. "We'll take care of everything. Go!"

I decided to call the police first, see if I could catch Chief James before he left for the day. It was almost four o'clock, and I needed to speak with the chief and then get to the ball diamond for my nephews' game.

I dialed the police station's number and waited for it to connect. I got a recording that said if it was an emergency to hang up and call 9-1-1, otherwise to remain on the line for the next available staff member. Then I had to listen to cheesy elevator music, something that sounded like a cross between disco and country. Yeah, it was pretty horrible.

Feeling a little traumatized by the music, I was relieved when a human voice came on the line. "Hi, this is Sunshine Baker at the library. I need to speak with Chief James right away."

"Chief has already left for the day," the bored-sounding phone-answerer said. "He had a personal commitment this afternoon."

My heart sank, but I wasn't willing to give up the fight. "No! I need to speak with him immediately!" I demanded. How could I take no for an answer at this point?

"Is it an emergency?" the man asked.

"Um..." Was it an emergency? Was it a matter of life and death? Not exactly, but... "You're holding an innocent woman in jail, and I can prove it," I blurted out.

"Again, ma'am, is it an emergency? Is someone going to die if you don't speak with a police officer immediately?"

I heaved out a breathy sigh. "Not exactly."

"I'll tell the chief you called," he said, not exactly comfortingly. "What was your name again?"

"It's Sunshine Baker," I repeated. "This is in regards to the library theft case."

"Alright, Ms. Baker. I'll pass along your message to him. What's the best number to reach you?"

"Does he have a voicemail?" I asked, thinking maybe he would check it from home tonight.

"Yes, ma'am."

"Can you connect me to that please?" I was desperate. As much as I hated voicemail and thought it was the invention of the devil, I was willing to use it if it expedited this process. Surely, if Susan was trying to get away with her crimes, she was simply waiting until the police were occupied with Evangeline and Jada, and then she would skip town. She had plenty of money in the bank now, after all. Plus all the cash she stole.

Then I realized that picture she had pulled up on her computer when I was in her office earlier in the week wasn't just a random picture of a tropical beach. It was a travel site. She was planning to go somewhere...maybe to the *actual* Cayman Islands?

The chief's voicemail connected, and now that I had put it all together, the words were rushing out at the rate of about three million per minute. "Hi, it's Sunshine Baker. I know you told me not to get involved, but...oops! Too late! My boss, Susan Gooch, set up two of my colleagues, Evangeline Dupree and Jada Booker. I have proof. You're holding Evangeline right now in jail, and I have a feeling you're going to be called to Jada's house soon. You've got to arrest Susan before she leaves town!"

So...I couldn't get ahold of Chief James. *What to do now?* Panic was cascading through my blood like a raging river during a flood, but I was desperately trying to keep my cool. *Maybe I should run over to Jada's house after all, so I can look for more evidence with Molly?*

I rushed over to my desk and looked up Jada's address in our patron database. Molly already knew where Jada lived because she'd been over there for her housewarming party, but I had a family thing that day, so I couldn't go. Of course, I forgot to get the address from her before she left—I didn't think I'd need it.

After choosing this course of action, I wasted no time texting Molly to find out Jada's address. Clutching my phone in my hand while I waited for a response, I walked back over to where Liz was still working. "Any luck?"

"Almost got it..." She didn't even look up, just kept typing away. Anna had taken a seat next to her sister and was looking at something on her phone, her attention span clearly spent.

I realized I could look Jada up in our library patron database. *Duh!* So I went back to my desk and typed *Jada Booker* into the search bar. Her name popped right up. *Score!*

Then I looked closer at the entry, only to realize it was a post office box number and not a physical address. *Oh no!*

Glancing down at my phone, I tried willing it to buzz with a text from Molly, but that didn't work. My mind raced, scrambling for ideas about how to figure out where Jada lived. Sucking in a deep breath, I decided I'd have to go upstairs to see if I could get Jada's address from her personnel file.

"I'm going to run upstairs for a moment. Be right back," I said, walking back over to Liz. "If you find the check images, print them out."

She barely looked up from the screen. "Yeah, just trying to hack the right server. Give me a sec."

"Of course. I appreciate this!" I put two twenty-dollar bills down beside her, and I was pretty sure it was the best forty bucks I'd ever spent.

I didn't want to go ask my boss for Jada's address, but obviously the post office box wouldn't help me find her, and the fact that I hadn't heard back from Molly yet was starting to alarm me. I'd just have to bravely march into Susan's office, tell her I was running late for my nephews' baseball game, get Jada's address and get the heck out of there before she could say anything else. I also wanted to look for any clues that Susan might be close to making a break for it. I had a feeling once Jada was arrested, she would be fleeing the country.

I hurried down the hallway toward her office, which was across from the activities room. The executive office suite featured its own lobby, where Susan's assistant was stationed. I stepped into the reception area and noticed immediately that my boss's office door was shut. She usually kept it open at least a crack.

"I'm just going to ask Susan something real quick," I told Pam, her assistant.

"Oh," Pam said, shaking her head, "sorry, but she's already left for the day."

"She has?" It wasn't even quite four o'clock yet. She

was almost always here till five. "Did she say where she was going?"

"Nope, just said she had an appointment." Pam shrugged and smoothed her light brown hair with her fingertips.

"Did she say anything else?" I pressed.

Pam pursed her lips, deep in thought for a moment before her face animated with a memory. "Yeah, it was a little strange, actually. I told her I'd see her tomorrow, and she just gave me this weird look and then laughed."

Oh no.

"Is her office locked?"

"I think so," Pam answered. "She usually locks it up when she leaves for the night."

"Do you have a key?"

"You can't go in her office," Pam insisted, her eyes narrowing as she looked me up and down.

"She wanted me to drop by Jada Booker's house, but she only has a PO Box in our patron database, so I need to get her real address. I was going to grab it from her file." And that would give me an excuse to snoop around a little bit too.

But Pam wasn't having it. "Oh, I can get her address for you. Hold on." The fingers of her left hand hovered over the keyboard while her right hand made a few mouse clicks. "Here you go: it's 115 Primrose Court."

"Oh, okay. Well, thanks." I glanced down at my phone. Molly still hadn't texted me back. Maybe she and Jada were just chatting away, and she didn't hear her phone buzz.

If only I could think of a distraction to get Pam away

from her desk just long enough for me to grab the keys. I knew there was a ring of keys in the top drawer—I'd seen it several times. I was pretty sure the one with the green plastic was for Susan's office. I didn't know how I knew; I just did. I could see a key with a green plastic cover stuck in Susan's door with the other keys on the large silver ring dangling beside it. It was a mental image I just couldn't shake. Sometimes having a photographic memory was the best thing ever.

At that moment, I remembered I had a scratch on my wrist from when I was holding Paige, and Bond decided he wanted to be in my lap. He swatted at Paige to get her to move, and she freaked out, leaping off my wrist and slicing into me with her back claws. As I scrambled for something else to ask Pam, I picked at the scab on my wrist.

"Big plans this weekend?" I asked her as I felt the scab give way under my fingernail.

"Not really. If the weather's nice, I might plant some flowers," she answered with a shrug.

"Were you at the gala last weekend?" I continued, knowing full well she wasn't.

"No, but I'm just sick about what happened. I hope we don't all lose our jobs." She shook her head at the tragedy. "I heard they found the Bible, though, and will be installing it tomorrow back in the lobby where it belongs. There's going to be a small ceremony and everything."

I raised my arm up to see my handiwork, and, sure enough, a tiny crimson streak was running down my skin. *Sweet!* "Oh my gosh! I'm bleeding!"

Pam's eyes doubled in size when they landed on my arm. "Oh, no! Are you okay?"

"Yeah," I said, squeezing it to make it bleed even more. "Do you have a Band-Aid?"

"Uh...I'll go see if there's a First Aid kit in the activities room. I think it's in one of the cabinets."

As she started to get up from her desk, I started praying, *Please don't need the keys. Please don't need the keys!*

Pam was a heavy woman and moved slowly. I watched her trudge across the hallway to the activities room and then lunged for the desk, opened the drawer and snatched the keys before she even made it all the way inside the room. Then I had the door unlocked in record time. I furtively glanced around Susan's office.

It was completely empty.

SIXTEEN

My mind was spinning as fast as a Gravitron amusement ride by the time I staggered back to the reception area of Susan's office, where Pam's desk was. Her jaw dropped when she saw me standing there, the keys in my hand and the door to Susan's office open behind me.

"I thought I told you not to go in there?" she growled, throwing a whole box of Band-Aids at me.

I caught it and tore it open to snag one for my bleeding arm. There was a red streak all the way from my wrist to my finger now.

"What's going on?" I demanded as I slapped it on my skin.

"Nothing." She crossed her arms over her chest.

"That's a lie, and you know it." I stepped closer to her, unwilling to back down. She knew something, and I wasn't going to let her get away with playing dumb.

"Susan is gone," she said with a shrug. "She's not coming back. No one is supposed to know until tomorrow

—and—" she narrowed her gaze on me, looking like she was about to spit venom out of her mouth at me, "—if you tell anyone, you won't live to regret it."

"Did she threaten you?" I stepped closer still, hoping to break through. Why was she being loyal to her boss who had stolen the library's money? Who had threatened all of our futures?

A tear glistened in the corner of Pam's eye as she sucked in a breath and stared at me. She wasn't going to give me any more. Maybe she didn't know.

Molly, I thought, fear striking a blow to my heart. *What if she went after Molly? What if...*

"I've gotta go."

That was the last thing I said before flying down the stairs as fast as my legs could carry me. I had Jada's address, and now all I needed was the proof. Liz was packing up her things when I made it to the ground floor.

"Well?" I panted, trying to catch my breath.

"Everything you need is right here." She pointed to the printer, where a stack of papers waited for me to collect it.

"You're the absolute best! If I have anything to say about it, I will definitely be hiring you to work here this summer." I rushed over, grabbed the printouts, and raced toward the door, calling out, "Bye, Anna! Thanks again, Liz!" over my shoulder as I sprinted to the parking lot.

As a heavyset girl, I was not accustomed to running, but my body had been flooded with so much adrenaline, I didn't really have a choice. My legs were carrying me faster and faster before my brain had a chance to tell them to slow down. I was lucky I didn't trip over my shadow in the middle of the parking lot! I aimed the key fob at my Mazda from yards away, practically somer-saulted into the driver's seat and raced off toward 115 Primrose Court.

If I plan to keep up detective work, I'm pretty sure I need a stunt double. It's a little more physically demanding than my library gig.

I spotted Molly's car on the street not far from Jada's house. There were plenty of other cars and trucks parked along the sidewalk, which curved around Primrose Court, but I didn't know Jada well enough to know which was hers. And I couldn't remember for the life of me what Susan drove, but I had a feeling the silver Subaru with the Bryce Beach Public Library decal on the back window was hers.

This was not good. I could feel it.

And the fact that Molly never texted me back only made it way, way worse.

I sucked in a fortifying breath and marched up to the small porch. Jada's house was tiny—half vinyl siding, half brick, dark green shutters and a matching front door. A potted fern hung from a hook at the edge of the porch. What was it I told Molly about not being afraid because I voluntarily work with teens? Okay, this situation was way scarier than any teen I'd ever seen in the library, but I was going to see it through. My job, as well as access to litera-ture, information and programming for the entire community of Bryce Beach was on the line, and I wasn't about to be the one who dropped the ball.

I rang the doorbell, and my heart skipped a beat as I waited. And waited. I heard a scream come from inside, a blood-curdling scream that could only be produced when one's very life was in jeopardy.

It wasn't too late. I could turn and run.

Before I could consider that option any further, the door handle twisted, and the door creeped open. I was grabbed around the wrist and jerked inside so hard, I was sure my bones cracked.

"Get over there in the corner," a voice hissed.

Susan.

I held my hands up when I saw she had a small gun and was pointing it right at me.

"Go, now!" she screamed, waving the gun in the air hysterically.

Now, I'd never been on the business end of a real gun before. My mother, never fully recovered from her peace-loving hippie ways, didn't allow my brother and me to play with guns. Not that I ever wanted to, mind you, but River sure did. He would make everything he could find into guns. Legos? Guns. Lincoln logs? Guns. Two sticks tied together with string and tape? A big gun.

So, even though the adult side of my mind knew what was happening was real, and I was in a considerable amount of danger, the child side of me, the little girl buried deep within my forty-two-year-old self, declared this was all make-believe. And I just needed to play Susan's little game until it was all over, and the police came.

The adult voice inside my head scoffed because the police weren't coming. I hadn't been able to get ahold of Chief James, and there was probably less than zero chance he would check his voicemail now that he'd left the office. They said he had a "personal commitment." Actually, I was pretty sure his niece and nephew played Little League, so his personal commitment was likely watching them play ball. How ironic that I was supposed to be there too. Instead, I was doing *his* job.

Jada and Molly were huddled in the corner. Jada looked almost as ill as Evangeline was when we saw her a couple of days ago. Molly was shaking so hard, she couldn't even get her lips to work, but she said everything with her eyes. I knew her well enough to know she was begging my forgiveness for not being able to warn me that I was heading straight into a trap.

I shot her a look that said, *I have all the evidence we need in the car, so all we have to do is make it out of this alive.*

When she nodded, I was fairly certain we understood each other. *Never underestimate the power of nonverbal communication!*

"I'm glad you've finally shown up, Baker," Susan sneered at me once I cowered in the corner with the two others. Jada was in the middle, sitting with her back in the actual corner. Molly was on the other side, her knees pulled up as she sat on the floor with the skirt of her dress covering her legs. I took a seat on the other side and wrapped my arms around my legs for support. I hated sitting on the floor. You'd think I had enough padding that it would be comfortable, but no. It felt like my bones were going to push through my skin.

Once I got situated, I looked up to see that our boss was still holding us hostage at gunpoint. I'd often wondered what it would be like to have a little more excitement in my life, but this was definitely not what I had in mind. "What are you doing, Susan? I don't understand where all this is coming from!"

"Shut your mouth, Baker. I already told the whole story to these other two morons, and I'm not repeating it for you."

"Well, that's not fair!" I crossed my arms over my chest. "What makes you think you're going to get away with this?"

"First of all, Chief James thinks I'm the distraught library director who lost the entirety of my library's donations for the year. He thinks I've been betrayed by two of my employees, one of whom is a certified witch!"

IS there such a thing as a certified witch? I wasn't going to argue with her, but I was pretty sure she was making that up.

Something told me it was not the time to tell her I had all the evidence we needed to connect the dots. There were a couple of different routes I could take, but I thought I'd try a guilt trip to start out.

"Jada and Evangeline might have betrayed you," I tested the waters, "but Molly and I didn't. You asked me to investigate, and I did. I'm the one who found the Bible! And this is how you're repaying us? By holding us hostage at gunpoint?" I *tsked* and shook my head. "I really thought you were better than that."

A dark laugh spilled out of my boss's mouth as she surveyed the three of us. Then her steely gaze settled right on me. "You know, I really thought you, Sunshine Baker, were a total idiot, a woman people barely tolerated, even though you think you're all that. I pegged you for someone who always did what they were told, who went along with the crowd as they tried *so* hard to fit in.

"Let me guess..." she continued, clearly enjoying the way she was belittling me, "your mom always told you you're the most beautiful girl in town, didn't she? And she kept promising you one day your Prince Charming would come and sweep you off your feet. That day never came, did it, Sunshine? Because no man would ever want a stupid, ugly, redheaded librarian—" She sneered the last word like it tasted sour on her tongue.

"So I was basically right about you. You're a worthless piece of crap, and that's why you, your equally stupid blonde ditz of a friend, and this young fresh-faced idiot next to you are going to let me proceed with my plan. Either you do, or you all end up dead. It's your choice. But by the time the police find your rotting bodies, I'll be looooong gone."

I wanted to defend myself. I wanted to fight back with every fiber of my being after she said such horrible, nasty stuff about me. But I bit back my vitriol, my venomous words. What did Jesus say? *Turn the other cheek.* I was going to turn the other cheek, and in the end, justice would be served.

Our boss began to pace then, still waving the gun around and pointing it at us every so often as she continued her diatribe. "You know what, Sunshine? I was a lot like you when I was younger. I was a yes-man...er, yes-woman. I did what I was told. I dutifully went to college and got a job. I went to grad school and got a better job. I was just a stupid librarian too, once upon a time. And then I got promoted. I learned a lot from managing a department, and then the entire library. Do you want to know what I learned?"

We all nodded, and I began to pray that someone, anyone, really, *but preferably Chief James, Lord*, would figure out none of us were answering our phones or were where we were supposed to be. I was supposed to be at the Little League game, and Molly was supposed to go to dinner at her sister's house, and I didn't know where Jada was supposed to be—I thought she was on vacation this week, but I supposed her vacation was just another one of Susan's lies.

"I learned that people are stupid. Just plain, straight-up ignorant. *Willfully* ignorant. People are so stuck inside their little, peanut-sized brains that they never learn to think for themselves or to see what's clearly staring them right in the face. We spend our whole lives working, doing the right thing, and for what? So we can scrape together a little bit of savings and retire. And we work so hard and so long that we get what? Ten years? Twenty years of freedom if we play our cards right?

"But it's not even freedom—because we have to conserve. We have to penny-pinch. We have to live on fixed incomes because tomorrow isn't guaranteed, and if we have a whole lot of tomorrows, we might run out of money. And then what?"

Where was all this coming from? I had never seen Susan ramble on before. She was always so practical, so efficient. It was like she'd been demon-possessed and was spouting off complete and utter nonsense.

"I decided I'm not going to play that game. I'm sixty-two years old, and life expectancy in my family is not very long. My parents died in their late sixties. My grand-parents, even earlier. I lost my pension at the library a few years ago when the board voted to do away with them and reinvest that money in other 'municipal inter-ests' like repairing the boardwalk, fixing our streets, and, yes, even expanding the police force.

"So, who's getting my pension? Chief James, for one." She rolled her eyes and stuck her finger down her throat, mock-gagging like she'd just stepped back in time. I was so tempted to tell her 1984 called and wanted their clichéd gesture back, but I somehow refrained from blurting that out. Self-control is a fruit of the Spirit, right?

"I took matters into my own hands," she continued. "Took me two years to plan. And I knew Evangeline and Jada would be the perfect scapegoats. Sorry, ladies."

"So now what?" I finally butted in. Speaking of butts, mine really hurt from sitting on the floor, and I wasn't sure how much longer I could sit here.

"Now, I'm going to leave. I'm going to the airport to board my flight to the Caribbean, where I'm going to retire with all the money I stole from the gala. It's right-fully mine, though, for putting my blood, sweat and tears into that place for nearly thirty years, starting out as a lowly reference librarian and working up the ladder—only for them to get rid of my pension and hang me out to dry. I'd have to work at least another five years to fund the lifestyle I really want, and I'll be dead by then. So, nope, screw that, I'm taking what's mine and heading off to enjoy my retirement just like I deserve!"

My instincts advised me to stroke her ego, go along with her story, let her think she was the mastermind of the best and most elaborate scheme in the history of heists.

"That's pretty smart," I praised her, nodding my head and looking at my co-hostages. "I don't blame you; that's for sure."

"When the cops come, they'll find all the deposited checks stamped with the library 'For Deposit Only' stamp—and it has your fingerprints on it, Jada. Remember last week when I asked you to stamp the checks that came in from the donors who couldn't make it to the gala?"

Jada whimpered quietly, tears streaming down her face as she rocked herself back and forth. Molly reached out and took her hand, trying to comfort the poor woman as an understanding of the situation she was now facing cemented itself in her mind.

"Jada, you're young, and this is probably your first offense. If you get a sympathetic jury, you'll probably only serve a few years. Just tell them all that student loan debt drove you to steal. And Miss Evangeline, well, I've been spreading rumors about her witchcraft for a couple of years now. Like I said, I've been planning this for a while."

So that explained why Willa Bryce Monroe adamantly believed our friend was evil!

I'd had my eyes glued to Susan this whole time, specifically the gun she gripped in her right hand. Using my peripheral vision, I caught Molly's motion to take Jada's hand. Then my eyes darted past Susan to the window looking out on the street. My phone had vibrated a few times in my pocket, and I hoped the calls were an answer to prayer. Squinting, I saw lights in the distance, and a wave of power washed over me, giving me the strength to do what needed to be done. I just needed to kill a little more time, keep Susan here for a few more minutes...

I drew in a deep breath, knowing it was now or never, and rose to my feet, my hands still up in the air. "So what about us?"

"Sit back down!" Susan screamed at me, her voice vibrating with adrenaline.

"What do you plan to do about us? We know the truth!" I taunted her. "And if you think we're going to let you get away with this...well, you're sorely mistaken."

Our boss's fingers trembled as she raised the gun toward me. "Look, I didn't want to shoot you. That wasn't part of the plan, but you just had to go and figure out what I was doing. You think Pam didn't call me as soon as you saw my office?"

She shook her head, clearly disappointed with us. "You and Molly were supposed to come over here, find the checks from the gala and the deposit stamp, and go straight to the police. The money is in an account that can't be traced to me. Once I'm out of here, no one will ever find me. I've got a whole new identity waiting for me."

Red and blue lights started to swirl around the room, and I had no idea how she didn't see them.

I knew I shouldn't say it...

It was a very dumb thing for me to do.

"Oh, you mean 'Gus Schoona'?" I retorted.

That was all it took. Like it was happening in slow

motion, I watched her finger lower and rest on the trigger, and I dropped back down to my butt, covering Molly and Jada with my ample body. The shot hit the wall, then another hit the ceiling as police slammed into the door, breaching the entrance. Drywall dust rained down on us as heavy footsteps sounded across Jada's hardwood floors.

"Everyone, hands in the air!" came the bellowing voice of an officer. He was flanked by another officer, and behind them was Chief James.

He'd come just in time.

SEVENTEEN

I didn't make it to the ball field to catch my nephews' Little League game that night. I was too busy going through the evidence Liz Cooper had collected on the account in the Cayman Islands.

Unsurprisingly, the police found a fake, but rather legit-looking passport in the name of Gus Schoona, as well as a boarding pass matching that name in Susan's phone. Gus was listed as male, so evidently she was planning to cross-dress as she fled the country. How she was able to pull off getting that passport was still a mystery to me, but she did tell us she'd been planning this for two years.

"Actually, if she hadn't launched into this huge confession, telling us in excruciating detail why she did it, she probably could have made it to the airport before you got here," I shared with Chief James as he wrapped up taking my statement.

I looked around the police station at the gray walls. It

was growing on me. This place was starting to feel like home.

"You did good, Ms. Baker," he said. "How did you figure out Gus Schoona was an anagram for Susan Gooch?"

"I saw an anagram book pulled out of her bookcase. It wasn't pushed in and aligned with the other book spines. That's the type of thing that gives a librarian nightmares, you know."

Chief James chuckled. "Well, you were a big help in this case, Ms. Baker—"

"Don't you think we should be on a first-name basis by now?" I teased him. He was starting to grow on me too...like the gray walls. He was like a gray wall that once *really* annoyed me but now was only *slightly* annoying.

"I was going to add a BUT," he said, leveling his gaze on me.

"Oh. So I shouldn't call you Vin, then?" I had overheard his parents calling him that at the gala and thought it was sweet. But as soon as that nickname came out of my mouth, his lips pursed. "Vincent, maybe?" I offered, using his full first name.

"Why don't we stick with Ms. Baker and Chief James?" he suggested. "And why don't you stick to librarianship from now on, and I'll stick to solving crimes?"

I scoffed and crossed my arms over my chest. "If you say so."

I hated to admit it, but I'd had more fun this week than I'd had in years as a YA Librarian. Don't get me wrong—I loved my job, and I loved the young adult patrons who considered the library their second home.

Anna Cooper was amazeballs! And her older sister was out-of-this-world smart!

This week had been the most exciting week of my entire life.

I had led a pretty boring life, after all, being a single gal in my forties with two cats and living in a tiny little town where nothing ever happened. For once, something *did* happen. And I was right there in the middle of it!

I picked up my things and started to leave, but Chief James called after me, "Oh, uh…Sunshine, wait!"

I whipped around, not expecting my first name to come out of his mouth. He stood there, all tall and broad-shouldered, the fluorescent light reflecting off the smooth, dark skin of his shaved head. "Yes?"

"We're releasing your colleague…uh, Ms. Dupree?"

My face brightened. "Oh, that's great!"

"Would you want to give her a ride home? I'm sure you have lots to catch up on." His lips turned up at the corners as though he was amused by the potential of *that* conversation.

I couldn't help but laugh at this point. "Of course I will."

I waited for the snippy guard I'd met the other night to bring my colleague around to the front of the station. Evangeline still looked zombie-like, but I hoped I could bring some life back into her with Chinese food or pizza or whatever sounded good to her. I hadn't eaten dinner yet, and I was starving. Crime-fighting sure worked up an appetite!

"Took you long enough," were the first words out of Evangeline's mouth when she saw me.

"I love you too!" I threw my arms around her. She wasn't a very huggy person, but she humored me by squeezing back...a little.

"Well? Are you taking me home or what?" Her brows quirked as she studied me, likely surprised to see such an exuberant smile on my face.

"Pizza? Chinese? Mexican?" I ran down the list of restaurants we could visit.

"Hmmm, which dish pairs best with vindication?" She smirked and looked down the street toward the water. "Maybe that Italian place?"

"On the boardwalk? You hate being that close to the sand!" I joked.

She rolled her eyes and tapped her arm to draw attention to her glowing white complexion. "Well, at least it's dark outside, so I don't have the sun to contend with."

"You have me, though," I teased her.

When she stared at me, blinking, I added, "Uh... Sunshine? Get it?" I shook my head. "Wow, jail sucked all the humor out of you, didn't it?"

"Call Molly and have her meet us there," was all my little jailbird said.

When I glanced back down the hall, Chief James was still standing there, watching us. He gave a little wave before we pushed open the glass doors, and Evangeline got her first taste of freedom.

J ada joined the three of us in the small booth at the cozy Italian place on the boardwalk, Angelo's. She understandably didn't want to be home alone, even though her captor was now sitting in the city jail awaiting trial—where she might have been if I hadn't intervened.

"I have so many questions," she said, her head bobbling like she was dizzy and trying to reorient herself to the status quo once again. I couldn't blame her. I felt like I'd been the action star in a summer blockbuster, and now all the sudden, it was back to business as usual.

"You and me both, sister!" Molly added. "Were you guys both sick?"

Jada looked at Evangeline and then back to Molly. "Yeah, I came down with the nastiest flu after the gala. I was supposed to go on vacation, and then I was too sick to travel. I never get sick!"

"I was sick too!" Evangeline echoed, her face the most animated I'd ever seen it. "It took me a few days to really succumb to it, but wow...worst flu ever."

"Did Susan give you a piece of candy at the gala? Right after dinner?" Jada questioned.

"Yes! And I wasn't going to eat it, but it was chocolate and mint, and I thought it might get the fish taste out of my mouth," Evangeline explained.

"You were both sitting at her table, weren't you?" I remembered, calling once more on my old friend, my photographic memory.

"Yes! She had public services at one table and tech services at another with her," Molly added.

"I bet the candies were laced with germs," I ventured.

"You think so? What kind of evil, twisted, sick person does something like that?" Jada shrieked. "And why? I don't understand her reasoning."

"I guess so she could plant the evidence?" Molly shrugged. "I have no idea, really. It's so strange..."

Evangeline huffed, "To keep us from talking about it at work, I bet."

"What a sicko!" Jada threw her hands up in the air. "How would someone even get ahold of germs like that?"

"Hey, she said she'd been planning it for two years!" I reminded them. "I wouldn't put anything past her."

"Boy, she sure underestimated you, didn't she?" Evangeline put her arm around me in another unexpected display of affection. *She might end up becoming a softie after all this!*

I shook my head. "I honestly have no idea how in the world she thought she could get away with it. She really believed she could sail off into the sunset with the donation money and retire at the beach like nothing ever happened?"

"And stealing the Bible," Molly added. "It's all so crazy."

"She had to create a distraction," I pointed out. "Parts of her plan were brilliant. Other parts still needed some work. Kinda like every time I create a new YA program at the library. There are always kinks."

They all giggled, then a serious look took over Molly's face. "So Liz Cooper cracked the case for you?"

"Oh my gosh, that girl is incredible! She's really going places!" I sang her praises. "I need to do something special for her."

"I don't recommend baking anything," Evangeline teased me. It was all part of their relentless obsession with reminding me that I could never live up to my last name.

We finished up dinner, and I turned to my friends. "Well, my parents are blowing up my phone. I need to stop by there before I head home for the night."

"See you at church on Sunday?" Molly asked.

"You know it." I slung my arm around her and gave her an affectionate squeeze. "Stay safe this weekend, ladies."

The four of us chipped in for the tip and slid out of the booth, each of us stretching our legs, and one or more of us failing to stop a yawn from creeping up. It had been a long day. A long week. And it was finally over. I led the way out of the restaurant and out onto the boardwalk, where the nearly full moon was hanging over the Atlantic, its reflection dancing on the surface of the waves.

We said our goodbyes, and I was about to head to my car when I felt the ocean beckoning me. I turned in the opposite direction and walked toward the small opening in the dunes that were edged with a wooden fence. The tall grasses, withered from the winter but starting to come to life again in the spring, blew in the chilly night air, and the crashing waves whispered my name.

Next thing I knew, my bare feet were sinking into the silver sand, carrying me through the shifting granules until the earth firmed beneath my feet, solid from the water rushing up onto the shore. I held my breath as a white-scalloped edge of a wave rippled over my toes, sending a chill down my spine. And then I exhaled, letting all the tension and fear that had held me in its grips throughout the week rush out and be carried back out to sea on the rolling tide.

✤

I knocked on my parents' door twice before stepping inside. I could hear my parents arguing from the kitchen, no big surprise there. It was a civil disagreement, but their voices were raised. I couldn't tell what it was about, and I didn't care—as long as it wasn't about me.

As soon as they noticed my presence, both of their tongues stilled. They rushed to me, enveloping me in their embrace and making a Sunshine sandwich.

"We were so scared!" the words finally burst out of my mother's mouth as tears streamed down her cheeks.

"You're about to squeeze the stuffing out of me!" I joked, stepping back to see the relief on both of their faces.

"Sorry, sorry!" my mother apologized as she pulled away. "Do you want some cake?"

"I just ate at Angelo's," I explained, and both parents heaved an empathetic sigh. It was impossible to leave that place in any other condition besides stuffed. "How was the baseball game?"

"Well," my father began, "the game was great, and the twins won, but that's not really the best part of the night."

My eyebrow arched as I looked at my dad. "What do you mean?"

"Chief James's niece plays on the same team as the twins, and he was there cheering her on," my dad said.

As soon as the words left his mouth, I had a feeling I knew what came next.

"I was chatting him up between innings," my mother took over the story, "you know, the neighborly thing to do. And I asked him how the library case was going. And he said, 'Now that you mention it, I left work early today, so I better check in and see if I have any messages.' That's when he listened to his voicemail and realized you were in trouble."

"Wow." All I could do is get the one word out. *God works in mysterious ways, doesn't He?*

"I still can't believe Susan would do such a thing," my father said, cutting himself a slice of cake and pressing his fork into the moist, chocolatey goodness. *Why couldn't I have inherited my mother's baking skills?*

"I know," my mother agreed—yes, the excitement of them agreeing on something was not lost on me. "She always seemed so reasonable. So...sane."

"Definitely not sane," I blurted out. "If you could have heard her little soliloquy at Jada's house earlier. Whew! There were some serious mental health issues going on there. She actually thought she was entitled to that money! She'd spent two years plotting how to steal it."

"Wow," now my father was limited to a one-word vocabulary.

"Was Susan ever married?" my mother changed the subject. I could see her wheels were turning, and I didn't like the direction they were going.

"Never married," I retorted. "And don't even think of saying it—"

"I just don't want you to end up jaded and alone like her," my mother said. "You're forty now..."

"Forty-two," I reminded her.

It had been a long time since my mother had butted into my love life—or lack thereof. I supposed she thought it was fair game now that I'd endured a traumatic event. I still didn't think that gave her the right, but...I did understand her concern.

"I would just feel so much safer if..."

She didn't finish the phrase because she knew I wasn't going to like where she was going with that comment.

"Speaking of which," my father butted in, realizing it was time for yet another subject change—frequent subject changes were the norm in our family.

"What?" Both of us planted our gazes on him.

"The church hired a new interim pastor," he revealed, "since Pastor Marks retired last month."

"Oh, well, that's good news!" my mother exclaimed with genuine joy in her eyes. "What's he like?"

"Well, he's in his late thirties, and he's never been married..."

Oh no.

Not much of a subject change after all, it seemed.

EIGHTEEN

For the first time in over a week, it rained. When I woke up Sunday morning, it was to the pitter-patter of raindrops on my roof. My bleary eyes finally able to focus on the world outside my window, I took in the layers of gray clouds looming from the top of the sky to the horizon. And there were puddles in my backyard too. *Ugh.*

A glance at the alarm clock on my nightstand revealed it was already eight o'clock. Time to get up and get ready for church. Every fiber of my being wanted to pull the cover over my head and drift back to sleep, but then I remembered that going to worship my Creator, who had quite literally saved my butt just two days before, would probably be a good idea.

I dressed in the sunny yellow and pink dress I'd worn earlier in the week to work, now that it was clean and pressed. I added a fuchsia cardigan to ward off the chill from the rain and patted Bond and Paige goodbye before heading out to my car. Church was only a few blocks away, but I couldn't be expected to walk in this downpour.

As I pulled into a parking space, I drew in a deep breath. *This is my family*, I reminded myself. *My brothers and sisters in Christ.* My gaze trailed over to the Bryce Beach Community Church sign in front of the stone building, which was only a few streets over from the boardwalk. It was an ancient building—though not the original church the Founding Fathers built back in the 1600s. That building had succumbed to fire, and so had the two erected on the same ground in the next two centuries. This particular church was built in the early 1900s and seemed to be standing the test of time.

Walking toward the building, I reveled in the miracle that the Founders' Bible had been recovered in good shape and was now safely ensconced in its new glass display case, complete with state-of-the-art security. Willa Bryce Monroe had seen to that. They'd had an official unveiling ceremony yesterday, in fact, but I was tired from my ordeal the night before, so I chose to stay home with my kitties and read. *I'm a librarian, after all. I can't be expected to people all the time!*

"Hey, you!" I heard a voice call out from behind me.

I whipped around to find Molly walking toward me with Evangeline and Jada trailing closely behind. Our other two colleagues weren't usually churchgoers, at least not at this church, so I was rather shocked to see them. But in a happy way, of course.

"Hey, ladies!" I called back, mustering a smile despite the drops of rain that were soaking into my sweater.

"Come on!" Molly encouraged everyone. "I'm getting soaked."

We all rushed up the stairs and through the two huge wood doors that formed an arch in the center of the stone edifice. And even though it was stark and gray outside, with no hint of the sun, the stained-glass windows in the sanctuary still looked vibrant with their rich colors and details. It was such classic architecture, it always instilled an instant sense of reverence when I crossed the threshold, like being transported to a different dimension.

"There she is, my Sunny Bunny!" my father bellowed from the entry to the sanctuary, where he and my mother were apparently serving as the greeters that morning. "Pastor Bethany!"

A tall man in a dark suit turned toward my father, and I got my first glimpse of our interim minister. He had short brown hair, a little thin on top; large, expressive hazel eyes with a thick brow; full lips and a healthy ruddy glow to his creamy skin. When he smiled, I saw his straight, white teeth.

He reached out to shake my hand. "Hello! I'm Pastor Paul Bethany."

"Hi, I'm Sunshine Baker." I felt the warmth from his hand seep into my skin. "Nice to meet you, and welcome to Bryce Beach."

"Sunshine Baker, what a wonderful name! I bet you like to bake, huh, Sunny?" He laughed and glanced at my father, looking for his approval.

My mother simply rolled her eyes. She knew his first impression left a lot to be desired when it came to sparking a romantic connection between us. He'd taken my name and stomped all over it. *Sigh.*

After he introduced himself to Molly, Jada and Evangeline, and my parents properly greeted them as well, my entourage and I made our way down the aisle to the pew where my family normally sat. My brother River and his wife Izzy were already there. My nephews were no doubt in children's church, which took place in another part of the building.

Then something happened I wasn't prepared for.

It started with a few people coming up to me and thanking me for solving the mystery of the stolen town treasure as well as recovering the library funds. Next thing I knew, there was a whole line of people waiting to shake my hand and congratulate me on a job well done.

As someone who had only ever lurked in the background—despite this red hair, big body, copious freckles, and the burden of an unforgettable name—I was in no way used to this amount of attention.

"Sunshine! We're so glad you were on the case, dearie," Willa Bryce Monroe said when it was her turn to pump my hand up and down enthusiastically.

She turned to Evangeline. "I'm still not so sure about you, but I'm glad you're okay and here with us today."

We all had a good laugh. Then Chief James's dark eyes pierced into me from the pew in front of us as he and his parents made their way to their seats. At first I didn't think he was going to acknowledge me, but then, right before Pastor Bethany made his way to the pulpit, Vincent James turned around and grasped both of my hands in his.

"Happy Sunday, Sunshine," he said. "It's good to see you."

I was in no way used to this amount of attention...

But it was definitely growing on me!

※

When I got home from church, I spotted Bond sitting in his spot in the window, soaking up the sunshine. I was so anxious to get inside and give my kitties some attention, I almost stepped right on a little envelope resting on my welcome mat.

I picked it up, examining it for clues. I just couldn't seem to shake this amateur sleuth thing! The envelope was plain white and had my first name neatly printed on the outside.

Opening it up, my breath hitched, panicking a little about what it could be. Susan had that nasty virus she'd infected my colleagues with. What if she had an accomplice drop this by to exact revenge for the way I'd foiled her scheme to abscond with the money and retire in a tropical paradise?

My fingers grazed over the smooth card, which had a watercolor print of delicate flowers on the outside. I opened it up to find the same neat printing:

Great job solving the case, Sunshine. You returned our Founders' Bible to its rightful place, and you saved the library. Thank you.

Wishing you well,

An *Admirer*

The word "admirer" was thicker than the others, like it had been outlined. What in the world was this about? Was it a trick? A trap?

Forty-two-year-old librarians who'd never been married and were—like Willa Bryce Monroe claimed—too pudgy to find a husband, didn't receive letters from secret admirers. I couldn't believe there was anything but a sick and twisted joke behind that card. I walked inside, stuck it in a drawer, and didn't think another thing of it.

Instead, I curled up on my sofa with Bond and Paige, and cracked open a brand-new book.

THE END

Collect all the clues at the end of each book to help Sunshine solve the mystery of her secret admirer.

Read the first two chapters of the second book in the Dangerous Curves series on the following page, or purchase it here now: Mystery at the Marina

Join my mailing list here and get a free book:
bit.ly/KLMontgomerynews

MYSTERY AT THE MARINA PREVIEW

N^o *o one fell asleep. No one left in the middle. I'm going to chalk that up as a win!*

"Thank you all for coming!" I called across the room as my patrons gathered up their things and began their mass exodus from the Young Adult area. My eyes followed the pack of teens, their low rumble of chatter fading away as they crossed the lobby and headed out the library doors.

"Make a wish on the Founders' Bible before you leave!" my voice carried into the lobby.

I witnessed several of my beloved patrons stopping to examine the ancient relic that was a vital part of our town's history. Having them make a wish on it was partially a ploy to highlight the priceless artifact's resurrection. And it was also to remind them the library was a place where wishes and dreams could come true. *After all, in books, anything is possible.*

I wiped the figurative sweat off my brow, though I

wouldn't have been surprised if there were a few drops of real sweat too. *Whew! Thank goodness that's over!* Planning and running YA programming was exhausting. I felt like a one-woman circus up here trying to keep everyone engaged. *But I think I succeeded?*

"Great job!" Anna Cooper clapped as she came around the wall of bookcases that separated the YA area from the adult area.

"You think it went okay?" It wasn't that I needed validation from my favorite patron, but... *Well, validation is nice, isn't it?*

"I had a lot of fun!" She set a stack of books on one of the wooden tables we'd used during the program and looked around. "Everyone leave already?"

"Yeah. They seemed happy, though? I think?" It was hard to tell sometimes with teens.

She nodded enthusiastically. And then: "Can I check these out? I know you're getting ready to close in a few minutes." Her big brown pleading eyes looked up at me. How could I say no to that face? Especially after she and her sister helped save the library just over a month ago.

"Of course, dear. C'mon over to my desk." She followed me, and I sat down to wield my trusty scanner, zapping the barcode on each one of the mysteries she'd chosen.

"Mysteries, huh?" My eyebrow arched as I peered up at her.

She flashed me a sheepish smile. "Yeah, to be honest, solving the Bryce Beach Bandit mystery was so exciting, I thought it would be fun to read a few mysteries too."

I had to laugh at her use of my phrase "Bryce Beach

Bandit." I'd coined it long before the newspaper interviewed me about my work to bust the thief of the
Founders' Bible and the proceeds of the library's annual
fundraising gala. Now the culprit was getting her just
desserts.

Mmm...desserts. I couldn't bake them worth a darn,
but I sure enjoyed eating them!

"I don't know what I would have done without you
and your sister. She's all ready to start her new job,
right?" I had hired Anna's older sister Liz to do some
website and other tech work for the library this summer. I
was anxious to see how it went, because if Evangeline
Dupree, my friend and our interim library director, liked
what Liz did with the YA web pages, she was considering
hiring her to redesign the entire library site. We needed it
desperately. Susan, our former director, was always
stingy when it came to technology. We'd had the same
website since around 2008. *Not good.*

"Yes, she's really excited to get started," Anna
confirmed. The precocious thirteen-year-old smoothed
her long braids over her shoulder as she waited for me to
print out her due date slip.

"You about done, Sunshine?" my best friend Molly
Simmons, the children's librarian, asked as she peeked
around the corner.

"Yup! Just let me finish checking these out to Anna."
I printed out the slip and stuck it inside the top book, my
usual routine. And then Anna stuffed the books in her
canvas bag—her usual routine.

"Have a good night, Anna. Tell Liz I'll see her bright
and early on Monday morning!"

Anna waved as she headed toward the lobby with her full bag slung over her shoulder. Books made her so happy that I could see the joy radiating off her as she bounced along in her cut-off jean shorts and sandals.

I turned to Molly, who looked like she was ready to burst with excitement, even after a long day of librarian-ing. *Not a word, but should be.* Her blonde hair was pulled up in a smooth bun on top of her head, and her summery sundress looked just perfect with a matching knit shrug over it.

"You look really nice today!" I gushed. "I was so busy getting my program together, I forgot to tell you."

Molly's cheeks flushed pink, and I knew right then that something was up with her.

"You look like you're excited about something more than dinner..." My voice trailed off as I studied her face, trying to figure out what was going on.

"I am excited about dinner!" she insisted. "But I have some other news too. I'll share it when we get there."

"Well, then maybe we all have something to cele-brate?" I suggested, and she pumped her head up and down in agreement.

We were going to the new restaurant at the marina. It was called Josie's Seafood Shack, and apparently "shack" was quite a misnomer. It was rumored to have taken over the coveted title of Most Elegant Restaurant in town, and it was perched right on the water with a stunning view of the docks at the marina as well as Bryce Cove and our famous lighthouse in the distance.

I followed Molly out to the parking lot, and when we exited the building, we both looked over our shoulders to see Evangeline coming down the front steps with Jada Booker, the head of technical services, falling in step behind her. The two were already friends before last month's Bryce Beach Bandit incident, but now they were thick as thieves.

Hmmm, maybe that's a poor choice of words considering what happened...

"Hey, wait up!" Jada called. She was quite a bit younger than us, still in her twenties, but Bryce Beach was a small town, and she probably hadn't found a clique to run around with. She'd latched on to Evangeline, who was in her late thirties, and Molly and I were the two old ladies at forty-one and forty-two, respectively.

"Are you guys hungry?" I asked as we convened in the parking lot. I was hoping we weren't going to stand there and chit chat when we could save the discussion for the dinner table.

"Yeah, let's go. I'm starving!" Evangeline dug through her purse for her keys. "See you guys there."

We all went to our cars and climbed in. My red Mazda CX-3 carried me down the main street of town and then down Mulberry until I arrived at the marina. I hadn't spent much time here in all my years of living at Bryce Beach, but with so many townsfolk raving about this restaurant, I had a feeling that was about to change. My parents came here for their anniversary last week, and I'd heard some ladies gushing about it at church the other day as well.

I parked, stepped out of my car, and smoothed down my navy blue skirt that was billowing up in the wind. Just what I needed to do was flash all the fishermen coming in to dock after a day out on the water. After looking around and not seeing any of my colleagues' cars, I assumed I must have beaten them there.

I waited on a bench in front of the restaurant. *Was I driving fast? How did I beat everyone?*

My thoughts were interrupted by two suit-clad businessmen walking down the front steps and heading into the parking lot. I shouldn't have been eavesdropping, but they were talking so loudly, I couldn't exactly turn off my ears. *That's not the way ears work.*

The shorter man, who was bald and looked to be in his mid-fifties with a salt-and-pepper goatee and thick black brows, grabbed the other guy by the arm. "I'm so glad we were able to work this deal out."

The taller man, who was a decade or more younger, had a head full of thick, dark brown hair. I couldn't help but notice he was incredibly handsome as he stopped and patted his companion on the back. "I knew we'd come to an agreement, Bob. There's a lot of money to be made, after all, and why not make it lucrative for both of us?"

They were stopped only three or four feet in front of me, apparently not caring if I overheard their conversation. And my ears still hadn't magically turned themselves off, so I kept listening. It was a good way to pass the time while I waited for my friends, who apparently drove like they were eighty years old. Either that, or they hit both red lights between the library and here.

"Exactly," the older man agreed. "And I have a feeling the fishing is going to be mighty fine this summer!" When he winked, the younger man laughed in agreement.

As they started to walk toward their cars again, I spotted my friends heading toward me from the parking lot. *It's about time!* I had to admit, though, I was still replaying the conversation between the two businessmen in my head. I wondered what kind of deal they'd made? *Something to do with fish?*

"Oh my gosh, do you know who that was?" Molly gasped as they made it to the bench where I was waiting.

I stood up to greet them. "Who? Those two guys?"

"Yeah!" She leaned in and whispered as though she was afraid they could hear her, even though they were clear across the lot by now. "That taller man is the mayor's son!"

"Mayor Steyer?" I repeated.

"Yes," Molly said, nearly swooning. "From the mayor's first marriage... I haven't seen him in years, but I'd recognize him anywhere."

Oh, right. I had forgotten that Camille Steyer, the chair of our Friends of the Library committee, was the mayor's second wife.

"Didn't he move away in elementary school?" Evangeline asked.

"He's back now, apparently." Molly shrugged. "I know that was him. He's cute, isn't he?"

Jada was still looking off in that direction. "For an older guy, he's totally hot!" She looked as though she needed a cold shower at this point.

"Who was the other man?" I asked Molly, who seemed to be a fount of information. *Why didn't I know that was the mayor's son?*

"I have no clue. Never seen him before." She shifted her weight from one foot to the other.

"Evidently, his name is Bob," I remembered from the conversation. "They were talking about some business deal. Something about how the fishing would be 'mighty fine' this summer."

"Hey, I'm still starving, you guys. And as your boss—"

"Interim boss," I interjected.

Evangeline shot me a scowl before continuing, "As your boss, I suggest we get going. We have a reservation, right? Aren't we running late?"

I glanced down at my watch. "Oh, fudgesicles! Yeah, we gotta go, ladies. Chop chop!"

We rushed up the steps and headed to the hostess station inside the restaurant after passing through the wide veranda. The restaurant was built as an addition to the main marina building, but it was designed to look like an old Victorian house with intricately carved woodwork painted in bright colors—pinks and greens. It was charming, and the smells wafting out from the kitchen made my stomach rumble.

The hostess was a young woman with her dark hair piled on top of her head, wearing a crisp white shirt and a black pencil skirt. She smiled, collected four menus and ushered us out to the back deck, which overlooked the water. It was a beautiful June evening, not too hot and not too humid. Really, the best weather you could ask for in the summer.

As we took our seats next to the deck railing, I saw a blue heron swoop down to the marshy area at the far edge of the marina. In the distance, the Bryce Beach lighthouse towered over the other end of the cove, guarding the beach. Our small town was anchored on both ends by land that jutted out into the Atlantic Ocean. On one end was the lighthouse, and on the other, the marina. It was about as quaint and cozy as a town could be, and I felt lucky to call it home.

"So...Molly has some big news," I shared as soon as we got settled in.

"Oh, let's order first," Evangeline insisted. "Otherwise I'm going to harpoon that heron down there and see if it tastes like chicken."

Molly rolled her eyes. "Gross. I can wait. It's not that big of a deal!"

The server, a young man with red hair and copious freckles—so, basically, one of my People, appeared just moments later with his notepad ready to record our selections. After he walked away, shaking his head because Jada asked him approximately three million questions about how the fish was prepared, all eyes turned back to Molly.

She laced her fingers together and brought them in front of her as she surveyed our anxious expressions. "Well... I'm adding a new member to my family," she announced, her smile so bright, it competed with the sun.

"Oh my gosh, you're having a baby?" I shrieked. *How in the world did she keep this from me?*

Her nose screwed up as her eyes narrowed. "What?! No! Not a baby." She chuckled, her hand flying to her chest as she realized the hilarity of my misperception. "A puppy, Sunshine. I'm getting a puppy!"

"Oooohhhhhhh..." I looked around the table and

observed unanimous smiles and happiness for our friend. "That's great. What kind of puppy?"

"He's a golden retriever mix," she said. "A rescue. I pick him up from the foster family tomorrow."

"Awww!" Jada cooed. "I bet he's adorable. Do you have a picture?"

Molly whipped out her phone and scrolled to a photo of a small puppy with long, fluffy gold fur and sweet brown eyes. "I'm going to name him Murphy."

My friends continued to fawn over the photos of Murphy, but my attention was rapt on something happening far across the cove. Near the lighthouse, I saw a large Coast Guard boat drifting alongside a fishing boat. *Hmmm, someone's in trouble.*

Despite growing up near the Atlantic, I hadn't spent a lot of time on or around boats. Not that I didn't have any interest, it just wasn't something I had much experience with. When I was in junior high, I had a two- or three-year stint when I wanted to be a marine biologist. I was pretty sure every kid went through that phase, but I was *super* serious about it at the time. My parents bought an annual pass to the aquarium, hoping to foster my interest. But then I got older and decided I was much too invested in books to abandon them for dolphins and whales.

Being here at the marina sparked that curiosity inside me again. I'd always wanted to scuba dive, swim with dolphins, explore an old shipwreck. *I'm too old for that nonsense now*, I decided. *I probably couldn't even squeeze this big body into a wetsuit!* I laughed to myself.

"What's so funny, Sunshine?" Molly angled toward

me. The server had just returned with a huge round tray holding our salads.

"Oh, nothing. Just remembering something funny from when I was a kid." I stared wistfully back out at the sea, still wondering what was happening on that Coast Guard boat.

MYSTERY AT THE MARINA, CHAPTER TWO

Saturday, it rained all day, but Sunday dawned bright, and I went to church as usual. Molly pulled in right behind me in the parking lot. As soon as she stepped out of the car, I knew something was wrong. She had dark purple circles under her eyes, and her usually glowing alabaster skin looked dull.

"What's going on?" I adjusted my sunglasses on top of my head to make sure they weren't obscuring my perception. Nope, she looked even worse once I took them off.

"The puppy," she practically growled. "He kept me up all night…"

"Oh no!" I thought back to the adorable photos she'd shown us of her new golden retriever mix puppy at the foster family's house. He certainly didn't look capable of causing anyone harm. "Are you okay? Where is he?"

She scrubbed her hands down her face. "He's in his crate at my house. Let's go inside. It's too…sunshiney out here. No offense."

At least she hadn't lost her sense of humor—she was still perfectly capable of making a wisecrack about my name. I gestured toward the church building, and we crossed the parking lot to the front steps. Our interim minister, Pastor Bethany, was right inside the door waiting to greet us. I wondered if the church elders were any closer to making a decision about making him permanent, or if he would be like Ryan the Temp from *The Office,* and someday just take over the whole church.

"Good morning, you ladies are looking lovely today! It's great to see you!" Speaking of sunshine, his face looked like a beam of solar energy had been projected right onto it.

"Hi, Pastor Bethany." I extended my hand to shake his and found his grip comparable to a wet noodle, limp and clammy.

He ignored me, instead focusing on my friend. "Is everything alright?" he asked Molly.

"Can you pray for her?" I answered for Molly when she flashed the pastor a nervous smile. "She got a new puppy, and it sounds like he's a handful."

"Well, of course!" He grinned. "God loves all creatures great and small!"

I thought that was a strange and somewhat flippant response to Molly's dilemma, but I was more interested in getting her inside the sanctuary and to our pew. She often sat with my family if her sister and brother-in-law didn't come—they were only sporadic attenders.

Molly sucked in a deep breath as I pulled her through the sanctuary doors and guided her to our pew. "He's so dreamy..." she sighed as she took a seat next to my sister-in-law, Izzy.

"Who's dreamy?" Izzy turned toward us, a curious look on her face.

"Pastor Bethany," Molly sighed again.

I thought he was a nice man and seemed to be a competent minister, but "dreamy" would never come to mind if I were looking for words to describe him. So Molly had a little crush on the new minister. That was sweet. Maybe she was too tired to keep that little nugget of info to herself. I'd try not to tease her too much about it.

I was getting ready to speak again when I felt pressure on my shoulder. I looked up to see Mrs. James, Chief James's mother, with her tiny, veiny hand on me. "Hi, Miss Baker. It's great to see you this morning!" she sang in her smooth, melodic voice that defied her age.

"It's great to see you too, Mrs. James!" When I stood up, I found myself looming above her, marveling at how she was nearly half my size, both in height and width. How someone so itty-bitty could give birth to a man of Vincent James's giant stature was truly a miracle. He obviously got his size from his father.

And speaking of her son... My brows furrowed as I looked behind her to find the chief of Bryce Beach Police looking like he was absolutely mortified that his mother was speaking to me. "Hi, Ms. Baker," he said, forcing his lips into a smile.

"Good morning, Chief James." We'd had a little quibble about whether or not we were on a first-name basis back when we...uh...collaborated? Not sure if that was the right word for the Bryce Beach Bandit case.

Guess we're sticking with formalities—even after all we've been through together.

He nodded as he waited for his mother to sit down before taking a seat himself. Then he turned to face the front of the sanctuary.

"What happened with Murphy?" I changed the subject back to the little canine tyrant who had apparently cost my best friend her beauty sleep.

"He's just..." She shook her head and sighed. "He's adorable, but he just wants attention all the time. And he doesn't understand the go potty outside thing yet at all..."

"Cats are so easy." I knew that observation didn't help my friend, but her woes only made me appreciate the relative ease of taking care of Bond and Paige Turner, my two cats.

"Yeah..." She pursed her lips and focused her gaze on the front of the church, where the service was about to get underway. The choir had assembled on the risers, with the music director poised to lead their performance. "I hope I don't regret getting him."

"It'll get easier," I promised her. My brother River and his family had a dog, a big English sheepdog. They'd had a bear of a time getting the poor girl housebroken, but now she was perfect—though she was roughly the size of a bear. "Hey, do you want to take him for a walk this afternoon?"

Her face brightened for the first time since I first saw her in the parking lot. "Really? You'd come with me?"

"Yeah, maybe we can take him down to the beach. You've got a leash for him, right?"

"Yes! Let's meet at Lighthouse Park after lunch." She sounded thrilled with my suggestion, like it was the best news she'd heard since we'd recovered the library gala donations last month.

I patted her knee and smiled. "Sounds like a plan!"

✻

The afternoon weather was glorious as I parked my Mazda and stepped out, the warm June breeze rustling my auburn curls. I adjusted my sunglasses and straightened the flouncy three-tiered shirt I was wearing over denim capri pants. Molly whipped her little SUV into the space next to me, and I spotted a tiny puppy in the backseat. My heart immediately melted.

I watched her open the door and scoop him up after he came to the edge of the seat and stared down at the pavement, too afraid to make the leap. "Oh my gosh! Why does he have to be so cute?"

"I know, right? It's hard to get mad at him when he's so freaking adorable." She shook her head as she set him down in the grass next to the parking lot. He began to tug on the leash, jerking her forward. "And he's so strong for the whopping fifteen pounds he weighs!"

"Let's take him down by the water. Retrievers love water, right?" I didn't know how I knew that, having never owned a dog or studied dog breeds, but I did. *Sometimes librarians just know things. We don't know how, but we do. It's one heck of a job perk.*

"They're supposed to." She tried to guide the tiny fuzzball down the path between the thick, scrubby bushes that grew at the edge of the parking lot, but he was insistent on sniffing every square inch.

We finally coaxed the little guy down the path, onto the sand, which he was very unsure of at first. That little nose went wild, though, checking out the myriad odors that belonged to the sand, water and just nature in general.

"So, what did you think of Jada's news?" Molly asked as we made our way toward the surf. Murphy ran into the receding water and then right back out again when another wave rolled toward shore.

"Oh, that she's dating Carlton Boxbury?" I had almost forgotten, that was how much thought I'd put into it.

"Yeah," Molly continued, trying to guide Murphy away from a dead fish that had washed up onshore. "Eww, no, Murphy!"

I had to laugh. "They sure like all the gross stuff, don't they?"

"Ugh, I know. He was trying to sniff his own poop last night." She rolled her eyes. "Do you know anything about Carlton's family?"

I shrugged. "Not really. I mean, they're not from Bryce Beach, so..." I kept my circle small. *Very small. Like it was barely big enough to be classified as a circle. More like a dot.*

The Boxburys lived in Moon Point, a community down the coast, south of our town. The Boxburys ran a massive seafood distribution center that served most of the Mid-Atlantic. And they were one of the wealthiest families in the area; I knew that much. There were rumors that Willa Bryce Monroe, the matriarch of Bryce Beach, had a brief affair with the original Carlton Boxbury back when her husband was still alive. That Carlton Boxbury was retired now. His son, Carlton Boxbury II ran the company now. And his grandson, Carlton Boxbury III, was the one dating our colleague, Jada Booker.

"Oh, I know, but his family has been around a long time. And they have connections to Bryce Beach..."

I knew by that she was referring to Mrs. Monroe, the wealthy widow who was highly revered in our town. She traced her lineage to Nathaniel Bryce, who founded the town back in the mid-1600s when he and some other folks looking for religious freedom sailed from England to the New World. They were headed to the Massachusetts colony, but were blown off-course by a massive storm, only to be shipwrecked off the coast of Bryce Beach instead.

I was still trying to figure out why Molly was so interested in Jada's love life when my friend let out a shrill shriek. When I glanced up, I saw what startled her.

Several yards away from the dead fish she'd tugged Murphy away from was a whole lot of them, their decaying dull-scaled carcasses strewn across the sand. My hand flew to my mouth. "Oh my gosh. What happened to them?"

Molly plugged her nose with one hand and pulled Murphy away from them with the other. He was very interested in learning more about them, stubbornly tugging her back toward the nearest fish. "I've never smelled anything worse than that."

I was sure the hot June sun beating down on them wasn't helping in the odor department. They were an interesting sort of fish, a rusty reddish-orange on top and a silvery gray on the bottom. The smallest ones were about eight inches in length, and the biggest were a foot or more. They weren't small by any means, and other than being dead, they didn't look like they had been injured or half-eaten by something else before washing up on the beach.

Molly had walked Murphy all the way back over to the lighthouse, where huge rocks jutted out into the water. She began to lead him up the rocks, with the pup pointing his nose into the wind, relishing the breeze as it blew his thick golden-blond fur back from his face. I whipped out my phone and snapped a picture of her and the dog, and then I took one of the dead fish. I didn't know why or what I planned to do with it. It just seemed like a good idea at the time.

We walked the trail around the lighthouse, which led to the picnic shelters further inland, then we weaved our way back to the parking lot. Murphy seemed to be getting tired, as he kept stopping and trying to lie down on the dirt path, his little pink tongue wagging out as he panted.

"Think we finally wore him out?" Molly ventured as she scooped him up into her arms. His eyes fluttered open and closed a few times, and he licked her face.

"I don't know, but he seems pretty happy about it." Seeing how cute they were together almost made me want a puppy of my own. Almost. But then Paige and Bond would probably plot my murder.

So no puppies for me.

As I walked back to my car, I couldn't get the image of the dead fish strewn across the sand out of my mind. I swallowed hard and tried to redirect my brain to dwell instead on the image I'd snapped of Murphy and my friend climbing the rocks by the lighthouse.

What killed those poor fish?

Find out in Book 2 of the Dangerous Curves series, Mystery at the Marina!

Or get the first three books in the Dangerous Curves Boxed Set 1

Find out more about the series at www. cozychristianmysteries.com

ABOUT THE AUTHOR

K.L. Montgomery writes #bodypositive sweet romance, romcom, and cozy mystery. A librarian in a former life, she now works as an editor and runs the 5000-member Indie Author Support group on Facebook in addition to publishing under two names.

Though she remains a Hoosier at heart, K.L. shares her coastal Delaware home with some furry creatures and her husband, who is on the furry side as well. She has an undying love for her three sons, Broadway musicals, the beach, Seinfeld, the color teal, IU basketball, paisleys, and dark chocolate.

facebook.com/greencastles

twitter.com/klmontgomery8

instagram.com/k.l.montgomery

bookbub.com/authors/k-l-montgomery

amazon.com/K-L-Montgomery/e/B00V2IEEUQ

ACKNOWLEDGMENTS

Starting this brand-new series was rather daunting, and I have quite a few people to thank for helping me get it off the ground. First off, my husband, who has been cheering me on throughout my career, but he's been very excited and supportive of this endeavor—and he's way more interested in helping with mystery plots than romance! Haha!

Secondly, to my beta readers: Lisa, Lori, and Kayleigh —I really value all the feedback you gave me and know this is a stronger book because of your help. Thirdly, to my proofreader and friend, Tina Kissinger, I'm not sure what I would do without you. Thank you for being on my team! Last, but certainly not least, a special thank you and shout out to Colleen Noyes from Itsy Bitsy Book Bits, who has been an amazing friend and support for me, in addition to the best promoter ever.

ALSO BY K.L. MONTGOMERY

Dangerous Curves Series

Betrayal at the Beach

Mystery at the Marina

Shooting at the Shore

Poisoned at the Pier

Bribery at the Boardwalk

Homicide at High Tide

Romance in Rehoboth Series (romantic comedy)

Music Man

The Flip

Plot Twist

Badge Bunny

Wedding War

Stage Mom

Shark Bite

Contemporary Romance Standalones

Given to Fly

The Light at Dawn

Reconstructed Heart

Women's Fiction

Fat Girl

Green Castles

Nonfiction

The Fat Girl's Guide to Loving Your Body

Made in the USA
Columbia, SC
18 July 2024

38838445R00140